'You're Alanna Diamond,' Reece said as he slipped off the stool and stood up. 'My wife.'

His wife.

Alanna swallowed, her gaze dropping away from his handsome face as those feelings swamped her again, feelings that made her face grow hot and her skin tingle all over.

Alanna's head spun with the intensity of her desire, every muscle in her body stretched tight as a drum.

Try to relax, he'd said.

No way was she ever going to relax whilst in his presence. She had to find some excuse to leave him. To be alone.

WIVES WANTED

**When a wealthy man wants a wife,
he doesn't always follow the rules!**

Welcome to Miranda Lee's stunning, sexy new trilogy

Meet Richard, Reece and Mike, three Sydney
millionaires with a mission—they all want to get
married…but none wants to fall in love!

BOUGHT: ONE BRIDE

Richard's story:

**His money can buy him anything he wants…
and he wants a wife!**

July 2005

THE TYCOON'S TROPHY WIFE

Reece's story:

**She was everything he wanted in a wife…
till he fell in love with her!**

October 2005

A SCANDALOUS MARRIAGE

Mike's story:

He married her for money—her beauty was a bonus!

November 2005

THE TYCOON'S TROPHY WIFE

BY
MIRANDA LEE

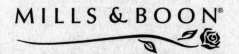

MILLS & BOON®

*First published in Great Britain 2005
Harlequin Mills & Boon Limited,
Eton House, 18-24 Paradise Road, Richmond, Surrey TW9 1SR*

© Miranda Lee 2005

ISBN 0 263 84185 5

*Set in Times Roman 10½ on 13 pt.
01-1005-39073*

*Printed and bound in Spain
by Litografia Rosés, S.A., Barcelona*

PROLOGUE

Sydney. September. Spring.

ALANNA hesitated at the entrance to the cemetery, dismayed to find that her stomach had begun to churn.

Just butterflies, she reassured herself, and forged on.

The churning increased by the time she stood in front of his headstone. But she remained determined to do this. To say what she had come to say. To find closure once and for all.

'It's been five years since I stood here,' she said to the man buried there. 'Five long, incredibly difficult years. I've come here today to tell you that you didn't win, Darko. I have survived.

'Time does have amazing healing powers and I finally found the will to go on, a will much stronger than I ever believed I had. I have taken my life in my hands. *My* hands,' she repeated quite forcefully as those same hands gripped her handbag in front of her.

'I've remarried, Darko. Yes, you heard me. I am now another man's wife. How you must be turning in your grave to hear that,' she bit out between clenched teeth.

'Of course, I did not choose a love match. Would I be so foolish as to marry another man who loved

5

me? But we like and respect each other, Reece and I. Best of all, Reece doesn't try to own me, or control me. He trusts me and wants me to be happy. He doesn't mind if I go out with my girlfriends. He doesn't mind if I wear sexy clothes. He even buys them for me. He bought me the suit I have on today. It's the kind of outfit *you* would have ripped off me. But Reece loves me to wear clothes like this.'

With a defiant tilt of her head, she spread her arms wide and turned around, showing off her eye-catching figure, encased that day in a cream silk suit that had a short, tight skirt and a figure hugging jacket with a deep V neckline.

'Did I mention that my husband is a very rich, very handsome man?' Alanna went on. 'Very sexy, too. He might not be crazy in love with me, but he wants to make love to me almost every night. To satisfy me. Which he does. Do you hear me, Darko?' Alanna threw at the headstone in a challenging tone, which didn't totally mask the underlying hurt and pain that twisted at her heart.

Tears threatened but she dashed them away. The time for tears had long gone.

'One final thing before I go,' she continued more calmly. 'Reece and I are going to try for a baby. Not every man is like you, Darko. Reece won't see a child as competition. Or something else to be suspicious of. Or jealous over. Reece doesn't have a jealous bone in his body.

'You will say that means he doesn't care about me. But you know what? I don't want to *ever* be cared for the way *you* cared for me. And you're wrong, anyway. Reece *does* care for me in his own way. And I care for him. He makes me feel good, something you never did for all your supposed loving.'

Alanna scooped in a deep breath before letting it out slowly, relieved to find that the churning in her stomach had finally subsided. 'My mother said I should forgive you, that there were excuses for your behaviour. But I can't do that. What you did was unforgivable. I am going now, Darko, and this time, I am never coming back. You are now firmly consigned to the past. And I will do my best not to think of you any more.'

CHAPTER ONE

THE organ player breaking into the wedding march signalled the bride was ready at last. She was only fifteen minutes late, Reece realised as he glanced at his gold Rolex. Long enough, however, for the groom next to him to get fidgety.

'It's showtime!' Reece said, smiling over at Richard who'd gone ramrod straight at the change of music, his hands clasped tightly in front of him.

'Have you got the rings?' Richard whispered out of the side of his mouth.

Reece patted the right pocket of his black dinner jacket. 'Of course. Relax, Rich,' he said, and reached out to touch him reassuringly on the arm. 'I've done this before.'

'So has he,' Mike muttered under his breath from the other side of Reece.

Reece's head whipped round to throw him a reproachful glare. Mike was a good bloke at heart, but his eternal cynicism over romance and relationships could be exasperating. It was also out of place today. Blind Freddie could see that Richard and Holly were deeply in love. This would be a much better marriage than the one Richard had had with Joanna, who, quite frankly, had not been Mrs Perfect.

Reece would never forget the night she'd made a

play for him, something he'd never told Richard, but which had bothered him greatly at the time.

He'd avoided Joanna after that.

When she'd been killed in a car accident a couple of years back, he'd felt very sorry for Richard. But Reece sometimes wondered if it was a case of fate being cruel to be kind.

Whatever, Richard's first marriage was past history. Today was a new day and Reece finally felt optimistic for his best friend's choice for his second wife.

Despite an initial concern that Holly, at twenty-six, was too young and naive for a man of Richard's age and status—Richard was thirty-eight and the CEO of a merchant bank—Reece could now see that Holly was exactly what Richard needed after Joanna. She was a genuinely sweet, caring, loving girl. Very pretty, too.

She was going to make a lovely bride.

Reece's eyes narrowed as he peered down to the back of the church, curious to see what the girls were wearing. But the church doors were open and the late-afternoon light was streaming in. All he could see were silhouettes.

The first bridesmaid eventually came into view, looking elegant in a long, straight red dress and carrying a bouquet of white roses. She was tall, with auburn hair, a nice enough figure and an attractive face.

Reece didn't know her. She was a florist friend of

Holly's. In her thirties. And married, Alanna had told him last night.

Reece hoped happily so, given she was being partnered by Mike today.

Reece glanced to his left at Mike, who was looking surprisingly debonair, a far cry from his usual dishevelled self. Amazing what a haircut, a shave and a tuxedo could achieve. Most days, Mike looked as if he'd walked out of a spaghetti western. Acted like that, too. Very tough and gruff.

Strangely, some women seemed to fancy him like that. Lord knew why. Reece thought Mike's clean-cut image today was infinitely more attractive. But what was one woman's trash was another woman's treasure, he supposed.

On Mike's part, he went for any good-looking female who made the chase easy for him and who agreed with his rules, his rules being he would take her out for one reason and one reason only. Sex. There would be no real relationship. No romance. The only promise he gave was not to be a two-timer.

But when it was over—meaning when he got bored—it was over.

Mike was an obsessively compulsive computer genius with a very low boredom threshold. His last girlfriend..an exotic dancer..had lasted all of a month.

It still never failed to astonish Reece just how many takers Mike got. And how many of his ex-girlfriends remained friendly with him, afterwards. Damned if it made sense to him.

'Behave yourself with your partner today,' he whispered in Mike's direction. 'She's married.'

'That never seems to stop *them*,' Mike returned drily. 'But don't worry. I avoid married women like the plague. They're nothing but trouble.'

'Sounds like you've had some experience.'

'Only once. It was a close call, but I managed to escape.'

'Anyone I know?'

'I don't think this is the time to discuss it,' he bit out.

Reece stared at Mike, who gave a slight nod in Richard's direction. Fortunately, Richard wasn't taking any notice of them, his eyes fixed straight ahead.

'Joanna?' Reece whispered.

'Yep.'

'She hit on me, too,' Reece admitted.

'No kidding. What a bitch.'

'Stunningly beautiful, though.'

'It's always the stunningly beautiful ones you have to worry about,' Mike muttered.

Just then, the chief bridesmaid came into view, dressed exactly the same as the girl walking a few metres in front of her.

Every male hormone in Reece moved from stationary into overdrive. Now *that* was one stunningly beautiful woman.

But, of course, he already knew that. He'd been married to her for nine months.

Reece struggled with a perverse jab of jealousy as he watched the eyes of all the male wedding guests slavishly following Alanna's graceful progress down the aisle.

Perverse, because he'd never felt jealous before, not even when she was showing off her model-slim figure in one of the revealing evening gowns he liked her to wear.

By comparison, Alanna was very modestly dressed today. Yet for some reason, the effect was sexier. Maybe it was true that what was hidden and hinted at was more provocative than what was on open display.

Or maybe it was the colour.

Alanna had never worn red before. She preferred softer, paler shades. But Holly had chosen red for the bridesmaids for some sentimental reason. Something to do with a bunch of red roses having brought her and Richard together.

The colour actually looked magnificent against Alanna's porcelain skin and creamy blonde hair.

The style was quite simple. A full-length sheath, it skimmed rather than hugged Alanna's figure. The neckline was wide. Almost off the shoulder, but not low-cut. The sleeves were straight and long, no doubt in deference to the weather. It was, after all, June. And June in Sydney was winter time.

The day outside was pleasant enough, but inside this rather old church the air was crisp and cold.

The first bridesmaid reached the end of the aisle and turned away to the side, giving Reece an even better view of his wife, especially her face.

And what an exquisite face it was. Classically

sculptured, with a delicately pointed chin, high cheek-
bones and a fine, fair complexion. Her eyes were a
smoky green, almond-shaped and lushly lashed. Her
nose was small and straight with an elegant tip. Her
mouth was full, her lips looking even fuller painted
scarlet.

Reece's gaze moved down further, his mind stripping her of that dress and seeing her as he liked seeing
her best of all.

Alanna had the kind of body that had always attracted and aroused him. Slender and firm, with long
legs, a tight butt and small, high-set breasts.

Body-wise, she was very similar to Kristine.

That was one of the reasons Reece has chosen
Alanna for his wife. He would never have considered
marriage to a woman he wasn't physically attracted
to, regardless of his motivations. The other, more
vengeful reason for choosing Alanna was that she was
even more beautiful than his ex-fiancée.

Her willingness to have his children was merely a
bonus.

As these thoughts tumbled through Reece's head
he tried to revive the vengeful feelings that had in-
spired his marriage to Alanna last year.

But astonishingly, they just weren't there!

Reece's shock was soon replaced by an over-
whelming sense of relief as he realised he didn't give
a damn about Kristine any more.

Let the devil take her, which he would.

The only woman he cared about these days was the
woman in red, coming down the aisle. His wife. The

stunningly beautiful, extremely enigmatic, very intriguing Alanna.

A few years ago, Reece might have believed his uncharacteristic jealousy a minute ago meant he'd fallen in love with Alanna.

But Reece had turned thirty-six this year, past the age when an intelligent man mistook male possessiveness for love. He did like and respect Alanna. A lot. But love?

No. Love wasn't what he felt when he looked at her.

Which was just as well, because love hadn't been part of their deal. In fact, it had been the one thing Alanna had been very adamant about. *No love.*

She'd been madly in love before, she'd explained. With her dead husband. The love of her life, killed in a tragic road accident.

She didn't want to tread that path again.

During their first dinner date Alanna had confided that she'd once believed she would never marry again, but as she'd approached thirty she'd realised she still wanted a family. What she didn't want, she insisted repeatedly, was romantic love, and all the emotional torment that went with it.

Which was why she'd become a client of Wives Wanted, an introduction agency that specialised in matching professional men of substance with attractive, intelligent women who were happy to be career wives. Although falling in love sometimes happened—according to the woman who ran the agency—on the whole, these were marriages made with heads and not hearts. Marriages of convenience, they were called in the old days.

A marriage of convenience was exactly what Reece had in mind when *he* had become a client of Wives Wanted a year ago. Love hadn't been on his agenda, either.

At the time, he'd got exactly what he'd wanted in Alanna. The ultimate trophy wife for him to display on his arm. The perfect salve for his bruised male ego. A visible token of his professional survival as well as a none-too-subtle weapon of personal revenge.

To this end, he'd made sure that photographs of his wedding had been printed in every paper and glossy magazine in Australia.

Not a difficult thing to arrange. He was a high-profile property developer, after all. What he did and whom he married made the news. Photos of every glamorous party he'd held since his wedding—and there were many—had found their way into the media as well, with Alanna always dressed to show off her physical assets.

For quite some time it had given Reece perverse pleasure to think of Kristine thinking of him with his beautiful blonde wife whilst she was having to service her ageing sugar-daddy, the one she'd dumped him for. He liked imagining his ex-fiancée feeling regret that she'd bailed out of their relationship prematurely. No doubt she hadn't expected him to go from near bankruptcy to billionaire status within three short years of her desertion.

Poor Kristine, came the caustic thought. If only

she'd had some faith and loyalty, she could have had her cake and eaten it too. Instead, she'd thrown her lot in with an ageing playboy film producer who had a reputation for replacing his starlet girlfriends every year or so.

There'd been a time when Reece had waited to hear such news with baited breath. Somewhere along the line, however, he'd stopped thinking about—and caring about—what happened to Kristine.

In hindsight, Reece could not put a date on this miracle. But it had to be some months ago. He supposed it was difficult to keep pining for another woman when you were married to someone as fascinating as Alanna.

Aside from her breathtaking beauty, Alanna was an amazing woman to live with. She never nagged at him or questioned him. There were never any scenes when he came home late, or had to go away unexpectedly on business. She kept his house beautifully, was an accomplished hostess and never said no in bed. What more could a man in his position want? When you thought about it, their marriage was perfect.

Frankly, falling in love would have spoilt it.

But as he continued to gaze at his beautiful wife Reece recognised that he *had* fallen in lust with her.

He'd always desired Alanna. Right from the moment he'd set eyes on her. But his desire seemed to have taken a darker, more intense turning today.

It was that damned dress's fault, he decided.

Not the style. The colour. It *had* to be the colour.

Red was the devil's colour. The colour of desire, and danger.

Whatever, Reece could not wait for Richard's wedding to be over. Could not wait to get that dress off her.

What a pity he was the best man and she was the chief bridesmaid. They would have to attend the reception afterwards, plus stay till it was finished. There was no excuse they could give to leave early.

Not that Alanna would. She would think him mad to suggest such a thing. She'd been helping Holly with the wedding preparations for weeks and had been very excited this morning.

Another dark thought intruded. Maybe he'd be able to persuade her to slip away with him somewhere for a few minutes. A powder room perhaps?

Reece had never done anything like that with her before. Their lovemaking had always been confined to the house. Actually, now that he came to think of it, it had also been confined to their bedroom.

Time to widen their sexual horizons, Reece decided with a rush of blood. *Before* she got pregnant.

They'd been trying for a baby for three months now. Surprisingly, with no success. But sooner or later, he'd strike a home run.

Reece imagined that once Alanna was having a baby, she might not be overly keen on having sexual adventures.

Suddenly, Reece became aware of Alanna frowning at him as she approached the end of the aisle.

Had his darker thoughts been reflected in his face?

Probably.

He swiftly summoned up one of his warmly winning smiles, the kind he used at work every day and which had become second nature to him.

'You look incredible,' he mouthed to her.

When she beamed back at him, his flesh tightened further.

Reece gritted his teeth and kept on smiling till she turned away to join the other bridesmaid, at which point his sigh of relief was swiftly followed by a jab of guilt. Damn it all, he was here today to be Richard's best man. Not to think and act like some depraved roué, consumed by uncontrollable lust.

The trouble was Reece had always been given to strong emotions. People thought he was an easygoing man, but underneath his charming façade he was often a maelstrom of emotion. Ever since he was a boy, his needs and wants had ruled his life. When he'd wanted something, he'd wanted it too much. When he'd fallen in love, he'd loved too much.

When Kristine had first left him, he'd gone wild with despair and jealousy. To the world, he'd presented a coolly positive, never-say-die image, whereas underneath he'd been eaten up by a compulsive need to strike back in whatever way he could; to have his revenge on the woman who'd spurned him. First, by regaining his wealth. Secondly, by marrying.

It had been sheer luck that his marriage to Alanna had worked out as well as it had. It could very well have been a complete disaster.

Now that Reece realised Kristine was out of his head and his heart for ever, no way did he want to risk spoiling things. He decided that, no matter how frustrated he was feeling at this moment, sex with Alanna could at least wait till they were home. Whether they got as far as the bedroom, however, was another question. He rather fancied the idea of undressing her in the living room. Or perhaps not undressing her at all.

He began to wonder what she was wearing underneath that red dress…

The arrival of Holly walking down the aisle was a well-timed distraction, dragging Reece's mind back from the erotic possibilities of later tonight to the sweetly romantic present.

He'd been right. Holly *did* look lovely.

Hearing the groom suck in sharply at the sight of his beautiful bride brought a wry smile to Reece's lips. Underneath his ultra conservative, buttoned-up, banker façade, Richard was a total softie. A romantic and an idealist.

A visionary, as well.

For which Reece was grateful. If it hadn't been for Richard's ability to think outside the box, *he'd* be stony-broke today. Richard had backed Reece when not one other financial institution would touch him. He'd given him every loan he'd needed till the slump in the real-estate market had changed to a property boom, extending his hand in friendship as well.

Reece thought the world of him.

'I admit I was wrong, Rich,' he murmured to his friend. 'She's definitely the girl for you.'

'Too young for him, I reckon,' Mike muttered, grunting when Reece jabbed him in the ribs.

'Okay, okay, she does love him,' Mike grumbled. 'I can see that. Even worse, I think he loves her.'

'What's wrong with that?' Reece said sharply.

'Hush up, you two,' Richard commanded. 'I'm getting married here.'

Reece gave Mike another savage glare. Mike just shrugged.

When Richard stepped over to take his bride's hand, Reece caught a glimpse of Holly's face through her veil.

The expression he saw in her eyes should have pleased him. For it was undoubtedly the look of a girl very much in love. Why, then, did Reece suddenly feel out of sorts? Surely he didn't envy Richard, did he?

Perhaps.

No woman had ever looked at *him* quite that way, with such gloriously blind adoration. Not even Kristine when she'd supposedly been in love with him. And certainly not Alanna.

Alanna, again…

Reece glanced over to where his wife was standing on the other side of the bride. But he couldn't make eye contact. Holly's veil was getting in the way.

Maybe it was just as well, he thought. Because he knew he'd never see anything like that expression in *her* eyes. The most he could hope for was a degree of mindless desire.

There was no doubt Alanna got carried away sometimes when Reece made love to her.

Reece vowed he would at least see *that* in her eyes later tonight. It wouldn't be quite as good, but it would have to do.

CHAPTER TWO

'You see?' Alanna said, smiling up into Mike's face. 'You *can* dance. In fact, you have a great sense of rhythm.'

Alanna had become tired of Mike always making excuses not to come to their parties, having suspected it was because he couldn't dance. When she saw him sitting down by himself at the bridal table, looking glum whilst everyone else was up on their feet, she'd decided to take matters into her own hands. So she'd sent Reece off to dance with Sara whilst she'd dragged Mike onto the dance floor.

The function centre Richard and Holly had chosen for their wedding reception was a converted Edwardian mansion that was simply huge, with polished wooden floors just made for dancing.

'You're a good teacher,' Mike said, glancing up from his feet at last.

'You're a fast learner. Now you can take your girl-friend out dancing.'

'Don't have one at the moment.'

'Oh? That's not like you.'

'Been working too hard.'

'On anything special?'

'A new anti-virus, anti-spy program. It's going to make me a fortune. Or it will,' he added, 'if and when

I can get the right company to market and distribute it.'

'What about your own company?' Alanna knew that Mike's software company had been very successful. Reece had shares in it. So did Richard.

'Not big enough. I need a top international company. American, preferably. With plenty of clout. I'll ask Richard to do the negotiating for me, once I decide who to approach. He's much better at that type of thing then I am.'

'But he'll be away on his honeymoon for the next month,' Alanna pointed out. 'He's taking Holly to Europe.'

'No sweat. The program's not quite ready. It needs more testing. Make sure there aren't any bugs.'

'I see.' Sort of. Alanna was no dummy, and she was competent enough on a computer. She used to use a computer every day at work. Although she'd given up her job in public relations after marrying Reece—being Mrs Reece Diamond was a full-time career—she still paid all the housekeeping bills over the internet. Nevertheless, she had no idea how computers really worked.

'I don't think Reece is too happy with you dancing with me,' Mike suddenly muttered under his breath.

'What?' Surprise sent Alanna's eyes darting around the room till she found her husband, who was still dancing with Sara. Even with his back towards her, he was easy to spot with his being so tall and having fair hair. When he turned around enough for their eyes to meet, Alanna was taken aback by the angry expression on his very handsome and usually cheerful face.

'Yep. He's jealous,' Mike repeated.

Alanna's hackles rose instinctively. 'Don't be ridiculous,' she snapped. 'Reece doesn't have a jealous bone in his body.'

'Come on, Alanna. Get real. You are one drop-dead gorgeous woman. If you were my wife, I'd be jealous of you being in another man's arms. Just because you two have a different sort of marriage doesn't mean a damned thing. You're Reece's wife and I'm a single guy with a certain reputation. It's only natural for him to feel threatened, even though it doesn't say too much for our friendship. He should know that you'd be the last woman on earth that I'd hit on. You and Holly.'

Despite Mike's explanation, Alanna still could not conceive of Reece being jealous of her in any way, shape or form. She'd danced with lots of men in front of him before, *and* wearing a whole lot less than she was today.

Not once had Reece ever criticised, commented, or cared.

As for feeling threatened by Mike…

That idea was equally ludicrous. Alanna had never met any man as confident or as self-assured as her husband. And he had every reason to be. Not only was he very good-looking and very successful, his personality outshone everyone else's. When Reece walked into a room, he became the sun around which the rest of the world revolved. Frankly, Alanna had never met another man quite like him.

'I don't believe he's jealous at all,' she pronounced firmly. 'Sara must have said something to annoy him.'

'Want to put it to the test?'

'What do you mean?'

Mike's hand in the small of her back suddenly pressed Alanna close against his hard male body, making her gasp.

The reaction in her husband's face was instantaneous.

His nostrils flared. His blue eyes narrowed.

Alanna's reaction to her husband's jealousy was also instantaneous. Chaos, inside. Chaos and panic.

'I don't believe this,' she whispered shakily. 'Reece is *never* jealous.'

'He's a man, Alanna. It comes with the territory.' Mike abruptly lifted the pressure on his hand and Alanna moved back to a more discreet distance.

'But he's never been jealous before!' she protested. 'You've seen some of the dresses he likes me to wear. Would a jealous man buy such dresses for his wife?'

'That depends.'

'On what?'

'On why he wanted you to wear such dresses in the first place.'

'I don't know what you're talking about.'

'Don't you?'

Alanna was taken aback. 'You'll have to be a bit more specific.'

'What do you know about your husband's past?' came the blunt question.

Alanna frowned. 'A fair bit. I know he's the eldest son of a family of three boys. I know his father died in an electrical accident when he was in high school. I know he worked weekends selling real estate from the time he was seventeen and was so successful he abandoned his plans to go to university. He told me he made his first million by the time he was twenty-one.'

'That's not what I meant. What do you know about his more immediate past, the years just before he met and married you?'

'Well, I know he went through a horror patch, financially, a few years back. He told me he would have gone to the wall if Richard hadn't helped him out. But I suppose you're referring to his ex-fiancée, Kristine. Reece told me how she dumped him for some wealthy older guy during that time.'

Which was why, Reece had explained the first night they'd met, he was no more interested in romance than she was. He'd been madly in love, and been hurt, as she had. And he didn't want to go there any more.

Of course, Reece thought her hurt came from her beloved husband's tragic death in a car crash. Alanna couldn't bring herself to tell him the truth about Darko.

Which made her wonder if Reece had been totally honest with her as well. Did Mike know something she didn't know?

'So Reece did tell you all about Kristine,' he said.

'He told me *everything* about her.' How beautiful she was. How she desperately wanted to be an actress. How they were only three weeks from their wedding when she left him.

'I doubt it, Alanna. No man tells his wife everything, especially about a previous woman who did the dirty on him the way she did. Men have their pride, you know.'

So do women, she wanted to throw at him.

'What did she do?'

'You'll have to ask your husband that. I've already said more than I should have.'

'But I can't ask Reece something like that. *You* have to tell me.'

'Tell you what?'

Alanna whirled to find her husband standing right behind her, looking daggers at Mike.

'Your wife wants me to explain how my new program works,' Mike said without missing a beat. 'But she's much better at teaching dancing than I am at teaching computer-speak. Do you want her back now? I gather by that he-man look on your face that you do. Time for me to go, anyway. I'll just have a word with the bride and groom first. See you around, folks. Thanks for the dancing lessons, Alanna. They might come in handy one day.'

Alanna felt new respect for Mike as he walked away. Whilst she was aware he was a genius in his field, she'd never thought much of his social skills.

That little display, however, had been very clever. It wasn't easy to think on your feet like that.

As she turned to face her husband Alanna decided to tackle his seeming jealousy head-on. She knew she would worry if she ignored it. As for her curiosity over what Kristine had done to Reece... That would have to remain unsatisfied for now. No way could she broach such a subject with Reece. He would be angry with her for discussing him with Mike behind his back. And rightly so.

'Why were you glowering at me just now?' she demanded to know. 'Mike said you were jealous.'

For a moment, Reece's face stiffened, his square jawline looking even squarer with his neck muscles all tight like that. His nicely shaped lips, usually re-laxed and smiling, were pressed tautly together. As for his eyes... Alanna had never seen them so hard. And so cold.

But then he laughed, and the Reece she knew and felt safe with was back. 'Aren't I allowed to be a bit possessive of my beautiful wife?'

'Being possessive is too close to jealousy for my liking,' she chided, but gently. 'I don't like jealousy, Reece.'

Reece pursed his lips, but his eyes were smiling at her. 'Don't you, darling? Sorry. Blame that dress you have on.'

'*This* dress? That's silly. This is a very modest dress.'

'It's the colour. It does things to me. If you must know, I've been thinking wicked things ever since I watched you walk down that aisle,' he said, his voice dropping to the low, sexy timbre that he used during foreplay.

Reece was a talker in bed, giving her head-turning compliments and calling her 'Babe' whilst he caressed her and turned her on.

Her breath quickened just thinking about those times. He was suddenly thinking about them, too. She could see it in his face, and in his eyes.

'I want you badly, Babe,' he muttered under his breath. 'I don't think I can wait till we get home.'

His calling her Babe at this stage was not only telling, but instantly arousing, as if he'd turned a switch on inside her. Alanna opened her mouth, then closed it again, finding herself speechless under his by now smouldering gaze.

Reece had looked at her with desire before. Many times. But this was a different type of desire tonight. Darker. And infinitely more exciting.

Suddenly, the room around Alanna began to recede, till she was aware of nothing but her husband's eyes on her. Her lips fell slightly apart. Her mouth went dry. Her skin broke out into goose bumps.

Very dimly, she heard the music change to a slow, moody number.

Without saying another word, Reece drew her into his arms, his eyes not leaving hers as he let them do his talking for him for a while. As he pressed her stomach against his stark arousal the most exquisite sensations gripped Alanna's body. Her nipples hardened. Her belly quivered. Her insides contracted.

Her arms slipped up around his neck and their bodies melded even closer together.

'I need to kiss you,' he whispered into her hair.

'You…you can't,' she answered shakily. 'Not here.'

'Where, then?'

She knew what he was asking her. It wasn't just a kiss he needed. The thought of him taking her somewhere relatively private sent the blood rushing to her head.

Even as she flushed possible places jumped into her mind. There were several powder rooms, a couple of them well away from everyone, on the first floor. Alanna had been upstairs with Holly the previous day, delivering her going-away outfit, so she knew the layout of the place quite well.

The temptation to go up there with Reece was acute. She wanted to. Far too much.

When she'd married Reece last year, Alanna had vowed to keep a tight rein on her highly sexed nature. No good ever came from a man thinking his wife was a whore.

She'd been quite content with their sex life so far. And happy in her marriage. Reece liked and respected her. Would he continue to respect her, however, if she let him do this? It worried her where such a surrender might lead. She wanted to be his wife and the mother of his children, not his married mistress, catering to his every sexual whim, regardless of time or place.

No. She had to resist temptation.

'I can't, Reece,' she said tautly. 'I have to go help Holly change into her going-away outfit.'

'She's dancing away happily at the moment,' Reece pointed out, nodding towards the bride and groom who were wrapped in each other's arms, gliding slowly around the dance floor. 'Come on. Let's go.'

'Go where?'

'You know where,' he ground out. 'I saw it in your eyes.'

She drew back and stared up at him, her heart pounding. Was she that easy to read?

'We're married, Alanna,' he went on brusquely. 'Whatever we do together is perfectly acceptable.'

'Being married doesn't make everything acceptable,' she countered heatedly. 'I'm sorry, Reece. You'll just have to wait till we get home.'

His face darkened with frustration. 'This is bloody ridiculous. You want to. I know you do.'

When his fingers tightened on her arm, Alanna wrenched her arm out of his hold and glowered up at him.

'Don't ever presume what I want to do, Reece,' she bit out. 'I said no. That means no. I don't know what's got into you tonight but, whatever it is, I don't much like it. Now I'm going to take Holly upstairs to change. Hopefully, by the time we get home you will have gotten over your caveman impulses and gone back to being the sophisticated man I married.'

CHAPTER THREE

THE strained silence in the car during the drive home gave Reece plenty of time to wonder, and to worry. He'd soothed his earlier frustrations with the surety Alanna wouldn't knock him back when they got home. But had his thinking been correct?

Alanna wanted a baby. Quite desperately, judging by her disappointment over not conceiving yet. She'd started reading books on the subject, and had circled the days on the kitchen calendar when she was most likely to conceive. Tonight was not optimum but it was close enough.

Back at the reception, he'd reasoned that no way would Alanna let this day end without sex, especially since they hadn't made love last night. She'd been busy with Holly on last minute wedding preparations whilst he'd been out having a few drinks with Richard and Mike. When he'd finally come home around one o'clock, Alanna had been in bed, sound asleep.

So he felt quite confident that some of his desires would be satisfied tonight. Although not all.

For a few seconds tonight he'd glimpsed a different Alanna, one who'd almost agreed to have a quickie. Her gorgeous green eyes had glittered wildly with the idea.

He wanted that Alanna to surface again. He also

wanted a wife who didn't lock the bathroom door after her any more. One who wasn't so darned protective of her privacy.

Such thinking revived his frustrations. All of a sudden, he wanted to snap at her. Taunt her. Challenge her.

Do you only let me make love to you because you want a baby? he felt like flinging at her. *Do you fake your orgasms? Do you care for me at all, or am I just a means to an end?*

Actually, Reece didn't believe she faked her orgasms. But there was *something* fake about Alanna. He just didn't know what. Up till this point, it hadn't bothered him how much of herself she'd kept to herself. As long as he'd got what he wanted, he hadn't made waves.

But everything had changed tonight. Reece wanted more from Alanna now, and, by God, he aimed to get more!

Alanna sat in the passenger seat of Reece's red Mercedes sports, her face turned away from him, her hands clasped tightly in her lap.

She knew Reece was angry with her. She could *feel* it. If there was one thing Alanna had become adept at over the years, it was sensing a husband's anger.

Not that Reece's anger was anything like Darko's. She'd trembled with fear when *he'd* been angry.

Alanna wasn't even close to trembling at that moment. But she was agitated. And upset.

She hated having made Reece angry. Hated herself

for her silly overreactions. He'd hardly behaved badly. So he'd been a little possessive of her. A forgivable sin, considering he'd been turned on at the time and she'd been off teaching another man to dance.

In hindsight, however, Alanna suspected most of his anger came from the fact that he'd witnessed her momentary willingness to go along with what he'd wanted. Seen it in her eyes, he'd said.

She'd acted like a tease. Going hot, and then cold, on him. No wonder he was mad.

She should apologise. She knew she should. But the words simply wouldn't come, and before long Reece was turning into their driveway and braking abruptly to a halt. He zapped the automatic gate-opener, then waited, his fingers tapping impatiently on the steering wheel till they opened.

Once again, Alanna tried to force herself to say something. She turned her head in his direction, but still could not find her tongue, gazing past him instead at the impressive façade of their home.

Every now and then—usually at the oddest moments—Alanna took a mental step back from her present life and tried to see it as others saw it.

All of her girlfriends thought her a very lucky woman. Which she was. She lived in an extremely beautiful home. Drove a snazzy car, and had a fabulous wardrobe.

But it wasn't any of these material things that were the main subject of her girlfriends' 'you-are-so-lucky' remarks.

No, it was Reece himself they envied Alanna the most. Her charismatic and very handsome husband.

Admittedly, he was a dream of a husband. Hard-working, cheerful, complimentary and generous. A great lover, too, who, till tonight, had not been at all demanding where their sex life was concerned. He seemed content with fairly straightforward lovemaking. In bed. Tonight had been the first time he'd wanted something different.

So, yes, on the surface, she was a very lucky woman.

But all that would mean nothing, she realised with a pang in her heart, if she never had a child.

Reece hadn't been the only person to feel unexpected jealousy tonight. When she'd accompanied Holly upstairs to help her change out of her wedding dress, Holly had confided to Alanna that she was already pregnant.

Alanna had done her best to express delight at the news, but, down deep, she'd been worried. Reece had been making love to her very regularly since she'd come off the pill three months ago, but still no baby. Was there something wrong with her? It was possible. You couldn't throw yourself out of a speeding car and not sustain some internal damage.

The doctors had assured her that she would be fine, that her recovery would be complete in time.

But maybe they were wrong.

Perhaps she should go for some tests…

'I presume you *are* coming inside.'

Reece's sharp words snapped Alanna back to the

present, where she was surprised to see they were already parked in the garages, the door had shut behind them and Reece had taken his keys out of the ignition.

'Yes, of course,' she said, and opened her door with a weary sigh. Clearly, Reece was still angry with her. 'I was day-dreaming,' she added as she levered herself up onto her red high heels.

'What about?' he asked as he climbed out also, banging the car door after him. 'Becoming a dancing teacher?'

His nasty crack shocked Alanna. He was never like this. 'You're not still going on about that, are you?'

'Why not? A man doesn't like his wife to enjoy another man's company more than his own.'

She stared at Reece over the roof of the Mercedes. 'I usually don't. But if you keep acting like this, I just might in future.'

'Meaning?'

'Nothing,' she muttered. 'I meant nothing.'

When she came round the front of the car and went to walk past him, heading for the internal access to the house, Reece grabbed her arm and spun her round to face him.

'I won't tolerate you sleeping around on me, Alanna,' he ground out. 'We might not love each other but we promised before God to be faithful.'

'I would *never* break my marriage vows,' she denied fiercely. 'But I might ask for a divorce if you keep manhandling me.'

He didn't let her go. Just glared down into her face, his own flushed and frustrated-looking.

'That won't get you a baby,' he snapped. 'Which is the only reason you married me, isn't it?'

'It was one of the reasons,' she threw at him. 'I told you I wanted a family.'

'What were the other reasons? My money, I presume.'

'I wanted security. Yes. But if you must know, I had no idea you were as rich as you were when I agreed to marry you. Now let go of my arm.'

He did so, but remained standing in front of her, blocking her way. When she stepped back a little, the front bumper bar of the car contacted her calves.

'What about sex?' he ground out. 'You said at our first meeting that you discovered you weren't cut out for celibacy. You implied you wanted a man in your bed every night for the pleasure he could bring you. Have I brought you pleasure, Alanna?' he demanded to know.

When she went to move sidewards, his hands shot out to grab her shoulders, holding her and forcing her to look up at him.

'Have I, Alanna?' he repeated harshly, giving her a little shake.

'You know you have,' she choked out.

It was cold in the garages, but her sudden shivering had nothing to do with the air temperature.

He yanked her hard against him, his blue eyes blazing like a pitiless summer sky. His mouth was just as pitiless.

Reece knew exactly the kind of kissing she liked. Right from their wedding night she hadn't been able to resist his kisses. By the time his head lifted, she was no longer shivering.

'Lie back across the bonnet of the car,' he commanded, his voice rough and thick.

Her eyes flared wide with shock. 'But…'

'Damn it, don't argue with me,' he ground out, then kissed her some more till all her defences were gone.

No protest came from her lips when he lowered her back across the engine-heated bonnet and started pushing her dress upwards. Up. Up to her waist.

Her heart pounded. Her skin flamed. Her head spun.

'Oh, Babe,' he groaned when he saw what she was wearing underneath her dress.

A red strapless corselette, with suspenders holding up her stockings, and only a wisp of a red lace covering her.

Her underwear had been a present from the bride. Not that she didn't like sexy underwear. She did. She just didn't usually buy red.

Reece ripped the lacy thong off her with a single yank, leaving her totally exposed. When he pushed her legs apart and leant forward, Alanna bit her bottom lip and squeezed her eyes tightly shut.

She tensed in anticipation of his mouth making contact, but it was his hands she felt first, touching her, exploring her, teasing her.

'So wet,' she heard him say, and knew it was true.

He made her wet so easily. Made her want to be made love to, even when she thought she didn't.

His fingers continued to play with her till she almost cried out to him to stop. She wanted his lips. And his tongue.

When he finally did what she wanted, her head twisted from side to side, her face grimacing as the exquisite sensations he evoked brought with them an equally exquisite tension.

His sudden abandonment had her eyes flying open.

'You...you can't just stop!' she cried out.

He laughed as he scooped his hands under her bottom and swept her up from the bonnet. 'Oh, yes, I can.'

'You bastard.'

His eyes glittered wildly down at her, his smile devilishly sexy. 'Tch tch. You're a lady, remember?'

'I don't feel much like a lady at this moment.' Her frustration was at fever pitch, making her almost violent with need.

'*Tell* me what you feel like,' he challenged her as he carried her inside the house. 'Tell me what you want me to do to you.'

Her already heated face must have gone bright red.

'You can say it,' he whispered wickedly in her ear. 'There's no one here to hear you but me. And I *want* you to say it, just the way you're thinking it right now. Go on. Say it!'

She said it.

'Don't worry, Babe,' he muttered, his arms tightening around her as he began mounting the stairs that led up to their bedroom. 'It'll be my pleasure to do that, and more.'

CHAPTER FOUR

REECE stared down at his still-sleeping wife, in two minds whether to wake her or not. It was Sunday and they had nothing planned for the day, knowing that they'd be tired after Richard's wedding.

But it was approaching noon, and she'd been asleep for a good eight hours.

Reece wanted her company.

Wanted her, too. The *new* her. The one who'd emerged last night.

His flesh prickled at the memory of the woman he'd unleashed with that episode in the garage. She'd become quite aggressive after they'd reached the bedroom, stripping him of his clothes almost angrily, wanting to be on top, wanting all sorts of things.

They'd had their first shower together some time later—now *that* had been a mind-blowing experience!—after which he'd refused to let her grab a towel, or a nightie, to cover her beautiful body. After a momentary hesitation, she'd stayed naked for him.

But it was like having sex with a stranger. She was nothing like the Alanna he'd become used to, his elegant and coolly composed wife who had to be almost seduced at times. This Alanna had been totally different.

Which Alanna would it be, he wondered, who woke up this morning?

Maybe last night was a temporary aberration. Maybe she'd had more to drink at that wedding reception than he'd realised. The champagne had been flowing and there'd been a lot of toasting.

Reece didn't like to think her passion had been alcohol-induced. He'd really enjoyed her reaching for him so avidly. He'd been thrilled that she'd kissed him for a change, and had wallowed in watching her make love to him with her mouth.

Damn, but he had to stop thinking about that. If he didn't, he'd be jumping back onto that bed with her.

Possibly, she wouldn't object if he did. But maybe she would. Reece's well-honed people instinct warned him to take it easy with her today; not to presume that there would be more of the same just yet. Alanna could be surprisingly touchy. She hated him to presume anything about her.

No, best he get himself out of here and go have some breakfast. The sun was up and it would be pleasant out on the back terrace at this time of day.

Rather reluctantly, Reece picked up the top sheet from where it was scrunched up at the foot of the bed and pulled it up over his wife's beautifully bare body. *Very* reluctantly, he let it drop onto her shoulders. A sigh whispered from his lungs as he wrapped his heavy towelling robe more tightly around his own naked body, then headed for the kitchen.

* * *

Alanna's first thought on waking was how great she felt.

Then she remembered. Everything.

'Oh, God,' she groaned aloud, clutching at the sheet as she glanced around the bedroom, wondering where Reece was.

Shock joined her agitation when she saw the time on the bedside clock. Twelve-fourteen! It was afternoon! She'd never slept in so late in all her life.

Admittedly, it had to have been the early hours of the morning by the time she'd passed out last night. Through utter exhaustion.

Alanna grimaced, then shuddered. What on earth had she been thinking about to act the way she had?

Of course, she hadn't been thinking at all. That was the problem. For the first time since their marriage Reece had broken through all her personal and sexual defences, whisking her away to that wild, wanton place that a much younger Alanna had enjoyed so much, but which she had subsequently learned could be a dangerous place for a wife to go.

When she'd married Reece, she'd vowed not to make the same mistake twice. Any man could fall victim to sexual jealousy, she'd worried, even a laid-back husband who wasn't in love with you.

And she'd been right! Look what had happened with Mike at the wedding reception. Reece had reacted, if not jealously at that stage, then very possessively. And that had been *before* her performance last night.

What would he start thinking now? Might he start imagining she was having affairs behind his back. She did have a lot of spare time with Reece working such long hours.

Alanna groaned aloud. What a fool she was to have let her husband open her Pandora's box. A stupid, stupid fool.

Alanna shook her head in dismay over the possible consequences of last night. No way could she live with any man who started acting even remotely like Darko. If Reece began questioning her about her movements, or doubting her word, or—God forbid—having her followed, then their marriage was history.

Maybe it was as well she hadn't fallen pregnant yet. She was still a couple of days away from entering her most fertile time so she doubted last night would have changed the status quo.

As much as the thought of leaving Reece distressed Alanna terribly, she refused to tolerate any scenario where her hard-won self-esteem and much valued independence was threatened. She'd come too far back from the abyss to be propelled back in that direction again.

But maybe she was worrying for nothing. Maybe Reece would be quite happy with the way things had turned out last night. After all, he was totally opposite to Darko, both in looks and personality. *And* he didn't profess to love her.

Now why didn't she find that last thought comforting?

Shaking her head, Alanna tossed back the sheet and made a dash for the bathroom. Afterwards she wrapped a towel around herself and returned to her walk-in wardrobe where she gathered together some clothes. Just jeans and a light jumper today. They weren't going out anywhere. Or entertaining, which might be good news or bad news, depending on Reece's reaction to her this morning.

Fifteen minutes later—Alanna never bothered with make-up or an elaborate hairstyle when alone at home—she was showered, dressed and on her way downstairs to the kitchen for some much needed coffee. At the bottom of the stairs she made a brief detour to peek in Reece's study, but he wasn't in there. Possibly he was out on the back terrace. That was his favourite place when the sun was shining.

As soon as Alanna entered the foyer, she could see that she was right. Reece was out on the terrace, semi-reclining on a banana chair, wrapped in his white towelling robe, sunglasses on, sipping a glass of orange juice and reading the Sunday paper. At his elbow sat an empty cereal bowl and spoon, along with the various inserts from the paper.

Alanna momentarily toyed with the idea of boldly going out there and saying good morning to him as if nothing had changed. But she was low on boldness this morning. She must have used all of her boldness quota last night.

Her stomach tightened as another memory assailed her. Had she really said those words to Reece when he'd first carried her from the garage to the bedroom?

Oh, yes, she definitely had. Maybe it was a rebellion thing. Darko would have washed her mouth out with soap. Literally.

But Reece had just laughed. Oh, how she loved him for that laughter.

Reece must have finally sensed her standing there, watching him, for his golden head suddenly whipped round. He waved the glass of juice up at her, then waved at her to come outside.

Taking a gathering breath, Alanna proceeded down the wide step that separated the foyer from the living area, bypassing the kitchen on the right as she headed for the sliding glass doors, and the terrace.

'Have a good sleep?' Reece asked as soon as she stepped out onto the flagstones.

'Wonderful, thanks. And you?' Oh God. She sounded awfully polite. As if they were hotel guests, meeting over breakfast.

He smiled up at her as he removed his sunglasses. 'Never better,' he said, tossing the sunglasses onto the side table. 'Pull up a chair.'

'I need to go get some coffee first. You know I can't think straight till I have my morning coffee. You want some?'

'I'll have whatever you're having,' he said, then threw her one of his megawatt smiles.

Alanna tried not to let the relief show on her face. But she felt almost overwhelmed by the realisation that everything was going to be all right.

'Just coffee to begin with,' she said, smiling back at him.

'You can't live on just coffee, darling. You'll start fading away to a shadow.'

'I'll have a proper breakfast later.'

'Would you like me to take you somewhere for brunch? We could catch the ferry over to Darling Harbour.'

'Haven't you just eaten breakfast?' she said, nodding towards the side table.

'Only juice and muesli. That's nothing. I seem to have worked up quite an appetite after last night. Lord knows why,' he added, his blue eyes sparkling.

He was teasing her, as he sometimes did. But never before had the teasing been about sex.

'If anyone should have an appetite this morning, it's me,' she retorted. '*You* hardly did a thing.'

She'd floored him for a moment. He knew she had. But then his sexy mouth widened into the wickedest smile.

'You saucy minx! But you seem to have a case of selective memory this morning. I distinctively recall you begging me to stop at one stage.'

'If that's so, then your hearing is defective, Mr Diamond,' she replied haughtily, thoroughly enjoying their repartee. 'I definitely *didn't* beg you to stop.'

'Oh? What were you begging me to do, then?'

'I *never* beg.'

'Every woman should be made to beg at some stage,' he said, his voice dropping low as it always did when his focus became sexual. 'It releases them from the women their mothers taught them to be, turning them into the women their husbands want them to be.'

'And what kind of woman is that?'

'The woman you were last night.'

'Not all men like that type of woman,' she said before she could think better of it.

'Such men are fools.'

'You…you didn't mind the way I was, then?' Alanna hated herself for sounding so vulnerable, but that was how she felt, all of a sudden.

Reece looked genuinely bewildered. 'Why on earth should I mind?' He put down the orange juice and rose to his feet, resashing his robe as he did so. 'I think I'll come inside with you whilst you make that coffee. I want to find out why you would think I would mind. And don't imagine you can lie to me, madam,' he said sternly as he took her arm and started ushering her inside.

'Would I lie to you?' she quipped, sounding cool and casual, whereas inside she was a mess.

Would she lie to me?

Too damned right she would, Reece decided.

For some reason, she hadn't allowed her real self to emerge till last night. He wanted to know why. And why last night? What had happened last night that was different?

The answer to that last question popped into Reece's head as he accompanied Alanna to the kitchen.

He'd been different. First at the wedding reception,

when he'd become all primal and possessive, and then in the garage, where his sensitive, new-age-guy persona had fled totally in the face of the most intense frustration he'd ever known.

It came to him that Alanna was one of those women who claimed not to like the caveman type, but who were actually turned on by them.

He would remember that in future.

'Well?' he said as he let go of her arm and slid up on one of the breakfast bar stools.

She ignored him for a few seconds as she went about turning on the kettle and getting herself a mug from the overhead cupboard.

'Well what?' she said at last, deliberately making her face a blank mask as she looked at him.

He rolled his eyes at her. '*Why* did you think I'd mind about last night?'

Her shrug was nonchalant. 'I guess because I'm not usually like that.'

'No,' he said. 'You're certainly not.'

She stared at him, and he could have sworn he glimpsed a flicker of fear in her lovely green eyes.

'But it was great, Alanna,' he went on. '*You* were great.'

She visibly winced, as though the memory of her behaviour offended her in some way. 'You really mean that, Reece?' she asked him, her expression touchingly unsure.

He wasn't used to seeing Alanna in any way but coolly confident, and it touched something deep inside him. He'd never imagined she was a woman who

CHAPTER FIVE

ALANNA turned away to switch off the jug and pour the boiling water into her coffee.

Dear heaven, but she wished Reece hadn't followed her in here and started this particular conversation.

She'd begun overreacting again. Being touchy and silly, snapping at him and even implying that sex was out, which was crazy. Aside from it getting closer to the right time of the month for conceiving, she really wanted him to make love to her.

He'd looked startled by her attitude, and rightly so. She'd been lighthearted and flirtatious out on the terrace, then all prickly and prudish in here. Alanna found it frustrating that Darko was dead and buried, yet she was still letting him spoil everything for her.

The atmosphere in the room was suddenly thick with tension. She could *feel* Reece's frowning eyes on her. He must be wondering what kind of weirdo he'd married.

And I *am* a weirdo, she thought unhappily as she picked up the mug and moved over to the sink. A screwed-up, emotionally scarred, seriously warped weirdo!

Alanna was adding some cold water to the steaming brew and wishing she could take back the last couple of minutes for an instant replay when her husband's arms snaked around her waist.

'Oh!' she cried out, hot coffee slurping over the rim of the mug into the sink.

'Reece, what on earth are you doing?' she gasped.

A rather silly statement. She knew exactly what he was doing, his hands by this point having successfully slipped up under her jumper and over her braless breasts.

'Just ignore me, darling,' Reece murmured as his palms skimmed over her instantly hardening nipples. 'Drink your coffee.'

Ignore him! How could she possibly ignore him when he was doing what he was doing?

Oh, God.

Alanna's head went into a spin when his thumbs and forefingers took firm possession of her stunningly erect nipples.

Drinking her coffee was quickly out of the question. She just gripped the mug like grim death with both hands and tried not to drop it.

Finally, a moan broke from her lips, her head dropping back against his shoulder. His hands immediately released her by-then burning nipples to take the shaking coffee mug and drop it into the sink, returning to lift her jumper upwards till her arms went with it and the garment was gone, tossed carelessly aside onto the kitchen bench.

'No,' Reece commanded when she went to turn around. 'Stay right where you are.'

'But…'

'Hush up, Babe,' he said thickly, unsnapping the waistband of her hipster jeans and sliding the zipper downwards.

'But…'

One of his hands cupped her chin and turned her head around just far enough for him to kiss her mouth, his other hand sliding down over her tensely held stomach, then under the elastic of her panties. By the time he let her mouth go, Alanna was leaning back against her husband's chest and shoulders, wallowing in the sensations his right hand was producing so expertly.

By then, all her earlier worries about there being consequences to her behaviour last night had dissolved to nothing. Clearly, Reece *liked* her like this. *She* liked herself like this, too.

How wonderful it felt to be finally free of the past, to be able to totally let herself go when her husband was making love to her.

Reece's left hand returned to play with her breasts, his outstretched palm skimming back and forth over the sensitised tips. She quivered with pleasure. Quivered and tightened.

Finally, what he was doing just wasn't enough. She wanted *him*, not his hands.

'Reece,' she choked out.

'Yes?'

'Oh, please… No more of that… Just…just do it. Please…'

'Are you begging, Babe?'

'Yes, yes, I'm begging.'

'Here?'

'Yes, here. Now.' And she began dragging at her clothes herself, pushing her jeans down her legs. Her panties as well. Soon, she was totally naked, her face flushed, her body trembling.

But when she went to reach for him, he would not let her turn around, keeping her facing the sink.

'Oh, God,' she moaned when his hands stroked down over her bare buttocks, squeezing them before moving down to push her thighs apart. She moaned again when his fingers stroked her open, making her slicker and even more desperate. Her bottom pouted back at him in the most primal invitation.

She cried out as he pushed into her, his flesh feeling thicker and harder than it ever had before. His hands gripped her hips as he set up a gentle yet sensual rhythm, making her whole body rock slowly back and forth.

Her head swam. Her heart thudded. She tried to catch her breath but could not. She began panting wildly. Her own flesh tightened around his, searching for release.

'Yes, Babe,' he urged. 'That's the way.'

She cried out when the first spasm struck, her knuckles turning white as wave after wave of pleasure swept through her. His orgasm was quick to follow, Alanna gasping when she felt the flood of heat deep inside her.

This was how lovemaking should always be, she thought dazedly. A man and a woman coming together as one. Passionately. Spontaneously. Uninhibitedly.

Reece was right. They were married. What did it matter where or when or how they made love?

When Reece wrapped his arms tightly around her and drew her back upright against him, Alanna's sigh carried total satisfaction with the experience, and the moment.

'You are never to hide this side of yourself from me again,' he said, gently stroking down the front of her spent body. 'Never. This is who you are, Alanna. A highly sensual women who needs to be made love to well.'

'Am I?' she said, still somewhat stunned by the experience.

'You know you are.'

The phone ringing splintered apart the atmosphere of tender intimacy that had wound around them like a warm blanket.

'We don't have to answer it,' Reece said straight away.

'But it might be important,' Alanna said after a few seconds. 'Your mother hasn't been well lately, Reece.' Reece's mother had developed type two diabetes, and had been having some health problems.

'Damn it, you're right,' he muttered.

'You have to answer it,' she said, already easing away from him.

He sighed as he wrapped his robe around his hips and resashed it. 'Yes, all right. But it had better not

be one of your girlfriends, wanting you to go somewhere today.'

Alanna scooped her jumper up from the nearby
benchtop and pulled it over her head, thankful that it
reached down to the top of her thighs. As liberated
as she was feeling, there was still something embar-
rassing about being stark naked in the kitchen in the
cold light of day.

'If it is,' she said hurriedly, snatching up the rest
of her clothes from the floor, 'tell her I'm indisposed
and have decided to spend the day in bed.'

Reece grinned at her. 'Wicked woman,' he said,
and reached for the wall phone.

'Reece Diamond,' he answered cheerfully.

Alanna watched and waited to see if there was
some problem.

'Hello, Judy,' he went on, Alanna's eyes shooting
ceilingwards at her mother's name. 'To what do we
owe this pleasure at this time of day?'

Alanna's mother often rang on a Sunday, but never
during the day. Always at night. It was cheaper to
call after seven. The country town of Cessnock was
hardly the other side of the world, but her mother was
a careful budgeter.

'Now you're being mysterious,' Reece said. 'Yes,
yes, I understand. She's right here. Just hold on.'

'Your mum,' he mouthed softly, his hand over the
receiver. 'With news for you which just couldn't
wait.'

Alanna's stomach contracted. The last time her
mother had had news for her that couldn't wait, it had

been to tell her her father had died, killed in a brawl outside his favourite pub one Friday night. That had been ten years ago, soon after Alanna had turned twenty.

'Is it good news or bad news, do you think?' she asked as she reached for the phone.

'She sounds pretty chipper to me. And very coy.'

Alanna frowned as she took the phone from Reece's hand. Now that didn't sound like her mother at all.

'Yes, Mum?' she said worriedly.

'I have some wonderful news. Bob asked me to marry him last night.'

'Wow!' Alanna exclaimed. 'That's great, Mum. Bob's a really nice man. Bob's asked Mum to marry him,' she relayed to Reece, who was standing there, an expectant expression his face.

'Tell her congratulations from me,' Reece replied, looking delighted at the news.

Alanna was genuinely delighted too, but surprised as well. Her mother had been dating the high school maths teacher for some time, but Alanna had always thought remarrying wasn't on her mother's agenda.

Alanna knew full well how hard it was to revisit a way of life that had previously brought you nothing but hurt and unhappiness. Her father had been a seriously neglectful husband, an uncaring, unloving man who had lived for his work mates and the pub. When drunk, he'd been very verbally abusive, putting his wife down, calling her names and generally being a foul-mouthed pig.

Alanna had despised and hated him, leaving home to move to Sydney as soon as she'd finished school at eighteen. She hadn't had much time for her mother back then, either. It wasn't till much later that she'd understood why her mother had stayed with her father all those years. Her own marital experience had taught her never to judge a person till you walked in their shoes.

'Tell her they'll have to come down to Sydney soon,' Reece called over his shoulder as he turned and headed off for their bedroom. 'We'll take them out somewhere special to celebrate.'

'Yes, I heard that,' her mother said down the line. 'And, yes, we'd love to. When?'

'I'll have to check my diary, Mum. You know Reece. He has a very active social life. I do know we're going to a party next Friday night, and an art exhibition on the Saturday night.'

'My, how do you keep up with him?'

Alanna laughed. 'Easily. I like to keep busy as well.' Which she did. Although no longer working, Alanna made sure her days were full. Of course, a lot of her activities were somewhat on the superficial side, but once she had a baby to look after that would change.

'You know, Alanna, your marriage to Reece has worked out much better than I thought it would. When you told me you were marrying a man you didn't love and who didn't love you, I was very worried. But once I met Reece, I knew you were in good hands.'

'*Very* good hands,' Alanna replied, thankful her mother couldn't see the erotic images that had instantly popped into her head. A wave of prickly heat washed over her skin, making her hotly aware of her still-erect nipples.

'Mum, I hate to love you and leave you, but I really have to go. Could I call you tonight? We can have a long chat about your wedding plans and everything.'

'I'd like that. You can tell me all about yesterday's wedding as well.'

'Yes, I'll do that, Mum. Around seven o'clock. Bye for now.'

Alanna hung up, then went to the nearest powder room, wondering as she washed her hands afterwards on how long it would be before she fell pregnant. She hadn't consciously thought of having a baby this time, which might be exactly what she needed to do. To stop thinking about it and hoping for it too much. Some experts said that stress and tension were some of the main reasons for infertility amongst couples. Often, there was nothing physically wrong with them. Some were just trying *too* hard.

When Alanna emerged, she wandered upstairs to the master bedroom in search of Reece, finding him in front of the vanity in their *en suite* bathroom, combing his hair. His bathrobe had been replaced by jeans, joggers and a pale blue windcheater that matched the colour of his eyes.

'That was a short call for your mum,' he said, smiling at Alanna in the mirror.

'I promised to ring her tonight. I couldn't stand there talking for ever.'

'Great. You're all ready to go, then?'

'Go where?'

'Out to lunch.'

'I…er…I thought we might stay home all day to-day,' she said, trying not to blush or feel wicked. He *liked* her bold, didn't he?

'That's a very tempting offer, Babe, but I doubt I'd survive staying home *all* day. I simply wouldn't be able to keep my hands off you and I'd be wrecked in no time. So I've decided we're going to drive into the city for something to eat.'

'The city? Why not Darling Harbour? And why drive? We could grab the ferry like you suggested earlier.'

'The city has more shops. I thought after lunch we'd look for an engagement present for your mum and Bob. That's why I want the car.'

Alanna's eyes lit up. She just *loved* going present shopping with Reece. He was not like any man she'd ever known in that regard. He loved buying things for people and didn't mind how long it took or how much money he spent. Christmas had been simply fabulous.

'We could buy your mum a little something at the same time,' Alanna suggested happily. 'Make her feel better.'

'Good thinking. Okay,' he said, giving his watch a quick glance. 'Now don't go getting thingy about your hair and face. You look great and we're not going anywhere fancy to eat. Just slap some lipstick on and grab a jacket.'

Alanna rolled her eyes at him. 'Oh, come now, Reece. No way am I going anywhere looking like this. Give me ten minutes at least.'

'Ten minutes and not a second more, madam.'

Twelve minutes later Reece's red Mercedes was heading for the city, the driver and his passenger in high spirits.

As they approached the first intersection at the bottom of their road the lights, which had been red, abruptly turned green. Reece could not have anticipated that the driver of a small green sedan coming along the street on his left would either ignore.. or not see.. his red light. A truck, parked illegally too close to the corner, blocked Reece's view.

His first sight of the car was out of the corner of his eye, registering a flash of green heading straight for Alanna. Reece yelled a warning as he pulled the wheel wildly to his right. But the green car still clipped the back of the Mercedes, spinning it right round and pushing it over into the path of traffic going the other way.

Suddenly, another car was heading straight for the passenger side, this one big and black and powerful.

Brakes screeched and Alanna screamed, Reece's arms stiffening on the wheel as he heard metal crunch with metal. When the side air bag exploded he prayed it had done its job.

But when silence finally came upon the scene and

Reece looked frantically over at his wife, his cry was the cry of desolation and despair.

For his lovely Alanna was unconscious, her head tilted sideways at an awkward angle, her skin deathly pale.

CHAPTER SIX

FOR one horrifying moment, Reece thought Alanna was dead. But then her head moved and a small, whimpering sound whispered from her lips.

Grabbing his mobile, Reece punched in the emergency number and screamed for an ambulance. By the time he finished the call, people had started crowding around the car, opening his door, asking him if he was all right.

'I'm okay,' he insisted. 'It's my wife who's been hurt.'

'Better not touch her, mate,' a man advised when Reece started to crawl over to her. 'Wait for the paramedics.'

Reece stopped and glanced back over his shoulder at the grey-haired man who looked around sixty.

'But..'

'I know, mate,' the man went on, his eyes soft and understanding. 'You love her. But there's nothing you can do for her right now. Best to wait.'

Reece slumped back into the driver's seat. He had never felt so impotent in all his life. Or so shocked.

Dear God, please don't let her die.

Reece kept on praying till the ambulance finally arrived, making bargains with God, promising all sorts of things in exchange for Alanna's life.

When the paramedic pronounced her in reasonable condition and not paralysed, Reece struggled not to burst into tears on the spot. Instead, he concentrated on helping them get her out of the car.

Prying open the crumpled passenger door proved impossible, so Alanna was carefully manoeuvred out through the driver's door and stretchered towards the waiting ambulance. Reece retrieved her bag from where she always dropped it at her feet, then followed her unconscious form into the back of the ambulance, leaving instructions behind for his car to be towed away.

By then, six tow trucks had arrived. So had the police, who were busily taking statements from witnesses, especially the drivers of the other two cars involved in the accident, neither of whom had been injured. One of the two sergeants involved, a big bloke named Frank, kindly told a distraught Reece to go with his wife and they'd catch up with him later.

Once the ambulance arrived at the hospital, Alanna was whisked away for X-rays and further diagnosis. Reece refused to be checked over himself, claiming he was perfectly fine.. despite an appalling headache and some pain in his right elbow. No way was he going to give anyone an excuse to separate him from Alanna.

But the doctor in charge of Casualty—a harassed-looking chap in his late twenties—was equally adamant. No one was to be allowed in with his patient at this moment. Reece would be called once his wife had been properly assessed and treated. He was advised to calm down and wait.

'Calm down, be damned,' Reece muttered to himself as he paced the waiting room.

But then he remembered his promises to God, and forced himself to get a grip of his increasingly wayward emotions. After making himself some coffee from the ancient machine in the corner of the less-than-salubrious waiting room, he sat down on one of the grey plastic chairs and waited.

The next hour and a half was unbearable. Three times, Reece surrendered to impatience and stormed out to grill the dour-faced triage nurse about Alanna's progress. Each time, he was firmly told there was no news as yet, and the doctor would send for him in due course.

By the time this happened, Reece was almost beside himself with worry, having convinced himself God hadn't believed his promises and something had gone terribly wrong. The look on the doctor's face only increased his concern.

'What is it?' Reece demanded to know. 'She's not paralysed or anything, is she?'

'No, no, nothing like that. Your wife has come round. She must have knocked the side of her head during the accident. She has a rather large lump in her hair above her left temple.'

'Then what's the problem?'

'The problem, Mr Diamond, is that your wife became hysterical when I said I was going to call you in to see her. She insists you tried to kill her in the car.'

'*What?* But that's insane! Why would she say something like that? Let me talk to her.'

'I'm sorry, Mr Diamond, but till I speak to the police I can't let you do that.'

'But I would never hurt Alanna!' Reece proclaimed heatedly, feeling both offended and confused. 'She knows that. Look, something's very wrong here. Maybe that blow to her head did something to her brain.'

'She's very convincing, Mr Diamond. Whatever the truth is, she *believes* you tried to kill her. And your unborn baby.'

Reece gaped at the doctor. 'But we're not expecting a baby.'

'She said she's only a few weeks gone.'

'I tell you,' Reece said firmly, 'Alanna is *not* pregnant. Give her a test. Find out for yourself.'

The doctor speared him with a long, assessing look, perhaps trying to weigh up who and what to believe. Reece knew then he would have to stay calm to get to the bottom of this madness.

'Very well,' the doctor said at last. 'Come with me. You can wait in my office while I do just that.'

'Fine.'

Another wait. Another test of patience. Another abysmal failure on Reece's part. Patience was not one of his virtues.

If he had any virtues at all, he began to wonder after a while.

When he'd been making his bargains with God back at the accident site, Reece had realised there were a lot of areas in his life where things could be greatly improved. Admittedly, he *had* baulked at promising to be a regular church-goer. The doer in Reece couldn't see that praying in a church every Sunday would be any great benefit to either himself, his family or the community at large. He had promised, however, to be a better man in general. In particular, he'd promised to spend more time with his ailing mother, to be kinder to his two idiot younger brothers, and give a decent amount of money to the poor and underprivileged.

Reece did already donate to several charities, but, to be honest, his donations were modest, unlike Mike, who spent a huge percentage of his earnings funding summer camps and buying computers for less-advantaged kids. Mike's obsessive drive to be successful had never been self-centred, unlike Reece's.

In the beginning, Reece had wanted to earn money to support his mother and his family, but somewhere along the line he'd begun wanting money for himself. Lots of it.

Okay, it *was* great to have money. He could not deny that. But Reece had found it meant nothing when faced with the possibility of losing the one thing of real value in his life.

Alanna. His wife.

'Damn, but where is that infernal doctor?' Reece grumbled aloud, jumping to his feet and pacing agitatedly around the doctor's small office.

When the door burst open a few minutes later, Reece whirled.

'Well?' he flung at the doctor, whose intelligent eyes betrayed bewilderment.

'You're right,' he said. 'She's definitely not pregnant. Not that I told her that. I suspect she wouldn't be too pleased with the news. I've given her a sedative and called the resident psychiatrist in to talk to her. His name is Dr Beckham and he's coming in straight away. Meanwhile, I really think you should go home, Mr Diamond. There's nothing you can do here.'

Reece reeled back from the suggestion. How could he just go home, without seeing for himself that Alanna was all right?

'Can't I just see her for a second?' he pleaded. 'From the doorway. Or through a window. Just a glimpse. You can be right by my side all the time.'

'I suppose that would be all right.'

The weirdest feeling of unreality gripped Reece as the doctor led him along the polished hospital hallway. He'd prayed for Alanna's life. He hadn't thought to pray for her mind.

The doctor stopped him at an observation window on his right.

'She's in there,' he said, nodding to the private room beyond.

Reece stood there, staring at the blonde head in the bed, using all his will-power to make her look at him.

His heart leapt when her head slowly turned in the direction of the window, his whole insides squeezing tight when their eyes made contact. If fear zoomed into her eyes, he didn't know what he'd do.

But no fear entered those somewhat glazed green eyes as she gazed steadily at him. Maybe a slight curiosity. But nothing else. *Nothing* else.

'She doesn't know me,' he said in shocked tones to the doctor. 'Did you see that? She doesn't *know* me!'

'Yes,' the doctor replied with a frown crinkling his high forehead. 'I did. Tell me, Mr Diamond, has your wife been married before?'

'Yes. Yes, she has. Why?'

'I wonder…'

'What? What do you wonder?' he demanded to know.

'Wait here for me. I won't be long.'

The doctor left Reece to go into the room and speak to Alanna. Soon, he was back, shaking his head in disbelief.

'I've never come across a case like this before,' he said, drawing Reece away from the window. 'I asked your wife for the name of her husband so that I could tell the police. That's who she thinks you are, by the way. The police. She says her husband's name is Darko. Darko Malinowski. Was that her first husband's name?'

'I don't know,' Reece was almost ashamed to say. 'I only know she was married.'

'Mmm. I'm going to have to call in another doctor as well as Dr Beckham. Your wife is going to need a neurologist.'

'I told you something must have gone wrong with her brain,' Reece said.

'You're quite right. Your wife, Mr Diamond, is suffering from a type of amnesia. She hasn't lost her entire memory. Just a big chunk of it.'

'Obviously the bit which includes me,' Reece said, his emotions swinging from dismay to a perverse kind of relief.

At least she didn't think he was the one who'd been trying to kill her.

But it did mean that she thought her first husband had. This Darko fellow. Reece couldn't remember the second name. But it had sounded foreign. Whatever, he'd supposedly been the love of Alanna's life. Yet she believed he'd tried to kill her and their unborn baby.

A relevant thought suddenly jumped into Reece's head.

'He was killed in a car accident,' he blurted out. 'Alanna's first husband.'

'Ah,' the doctor said, rubbing his chin. 'That could explain it, then. Was she with him in the accident?'

Reece grimaced. 'I don't know.'

The doctor's glance was sharp, plus a touch disapproving. 'You don't seem to know all that much about your wife's past,' he said, reinforcing Reece's discomfort.

Because he didn't.

But was that his fault, or Alanna's?

Probably both of them, Reece conceded. They'd gone into their marriage with their own private agendas which hadn't included confessing all to their prospective partners. Possibly because that kind of deep and meaningful discussion was associated with romantic courtships. People madly in love wanted to know everything about each other from day one.

Reece hadn't wanted to know anything much about Alanna's past at the time. She fulfilled his requirements for a wife and that was all he was interested in.

But everything had changed now.

'I suspect my wife kept secrets from me,' he tried excusing himself, whilst thinking he hadn't been much better.

He'd never told Alanna about that last awful day with Kristine; how the things she'd done and said had been like a knife in his guts afterwards, twisting and turning for such a long time. He certainly hadn't told Alanna that he'd initially married her as an instrument of revenge, that he hadn't even cared in the beginning whether she ever had a baby or not. He'd shown her off to the world.. and Kristine.. in a wickedly ruthless fashion, not caring a hoot for the real woman beneath the bright and beautiful façade.

Yet, somehow, Alanna had still crept under his skin, making him forget Kristine, making him care about her.

And now…now, she didn't even know him.

This knowledge was an even sharper knife in his guts, and his heart. What if she *never* remembered him? What then?

Last night, he'd craved to have her look at him with

mindless desire. And she had. More than once. Today, he would settle for her to just look at him with re-membrance in her lovely green eyes.

'For pity's sake, tell me this is just a temporary condition,' he said with a despairing look at the doctor.

'I wish I could,' came the considered reply. 'I did study amnesia, of course. The textbooks say that most trauma-based amnesiacs do recover their memories in time. But not all of them. On top of that, I have no actual experience in the field. You'll have to speak to someone with more expertise than myself. Dr Jenkins is the chief neurologist at this hospital. I'll have him called in to see to your wife and to talk to you. Now I am sorry, Mr Diamond, but I do have to get back to Casualty. I would suggest that you go home till Dr Jenkins calls you. It could be several hours before he arrives. If I recall rightly, he went down to the snow-fields this weekend.'

'Go home! You have to be kidding. Look, Alanna thinks I'm the police. Why can't I go along and sit with her till Dr Beckham arrives? She must be fright-ened being all by herself and thinking her husband just tried to kill her.'

The doctor didn't look entirely convinced.

'Isn't it better I be with her than nobody?' Reece argued reasonably. 'If she thinks I'm the police, I would be a reassuring presence. I could say I'm pro-tecting her. I promise I won't say or do anything to upset her.'

The doctor looked frazzled, possibly because he was needed back in Casualty.

Reece's frustration bubbled over. 'Damn it all, man, what harm could it do?'

'All right. But I'll be telling the nurses to keep a close eye on things. Your wife is in a very fragile state right now, Mr Diamond. If she starts getting distressed for any reason, you're out of there. Right?' he snapped.

'Fair enough.'

CHAPTER SEVEN

ALANNA was struggling to keep awake. Her eyelids were drooping and her brain was going fuzzy. That doctor had given her something.

But going to sleep was far too dangerous. Darko was out there somewhere, waiting for his chance to get to her and finish off what he'd tried to do in the car.

She kept her eyes fixed on the door and forced herself to stay awake, certain that any moment it would open and her husband would appear. Her only weapon of defence against him in here was her voice. She could still scream. But she couldn't even do that if she were asleep.

The doctor had tried to reassure her earlier that she was safe. But Darko was not a man to be easily stopped. She could see him in her mind's eye, convincing the police and the medical staff that his wife was the crazy one. Somehow, he would get to her. Somehow.

He wanted her dead. Her and her baby.

Alanna's heart almost jumped out of her chest when the door knob began to turn.

Her mouth opened to scream when one of the nurses walked in, followed by the fair-haired policeman she'd seen earlier with the doctor.

Sheer relief brought a small sob to her lips.

The nurse hurried over to the side of the bed, her expression caring and kind.

'This gentleman is going to sit with you,' she said. 'You don't have to talk, Mrs Diamond. Just close your eyes and go to sleep.'

Alanna frowned up at her. '*What* did you just call me?'

Worry catapulted into the nurse's eyes. 'Oh, dear. I forgot.' And she threw the handsome detective a frantic glance.

'It's all right, Sister,' he replied. 'A perfectly reasonable mistake. Don't worry. I'll take it from here.'

'Are you sure?' she returned.

'Absolutely.'

Reece shepherded the nurse from the room, having already decided that the best medicine for Alanna was to be told that she had lost part of her memory and that her obviously violent ex-husband was dead and buried. Much better all round than her worrying herself sick that he might come in at any moment for a second go at killing her. He'd seen the total panic in her eyes when they'd first come in.

The Casualty Doctor might think he had his patient's best interests at heart, but he obviously hadn't thought this situation through. Which was better? A shock or two, or gut-wrenching fear?

There was safety in the truth. Safety and security.

Reece closed the door of the hospital room and

returned to draw a chair up to the bed, his eyes scanning Alanna's face as he sat down.

How pale she looked. Pale and frightened and, yes, fragile.

Only then did he hesitate. Was she ready for such news? Could she cope?

The woman *he'd* married could. But this wasn't that same woman. Still, she had to know the truth. Anything else would be even more cruel.

'Are you feeling all right?' he asked her softly, thinking how beautiful she still looked, even with her skin an ashen colour and her fair hair all a-tangle around her face.

'I'm a bit sleepy. But you must tell me what's going on. What was it the nurse forgot?'

'Firstly,' he began in a gentle tone, 'let me assure you that you are not in any danger. Your husband can't harm you in any way any more.'

'You…you have him in custody?' she asked, her voice shaky, her eyes haunted.

Reece's hands balled into fists in his lap. If that bastard hadn't already been dead, he would have killed him himself.

'Let's just say he has no way of getting to you.'

'You might think that because you're here,' she said, her eyes still flashing with fear. 'But you don't know Darko. He's very strong and very clever. If he's still out there, he'll find a way.'

'He's not out there, Alanna,' he said, noting her slight surprise when he used her first name. But what else could he call her? 'Darko is dead.'

'Dead...' The word whispered from her lips, her eyes going oddly blank for a moment.

'Dead,' she repeated, then groaned as her hands whipped up to cover her face.

Her shoulders started shaking.

'He's not worth your tears,' Reece said, stunned that she would cry for such a man.

'I'm not crying for him,' Alanna choked out between her fingers. 'I'm crying because I'm safe.' Her hands raked down her tear-stained cheeks to clasp together in a prayer-like gesture below her chin. 'And so is my baby. I knew when I jumped out of the car that it was a terrible risk. He was going so fast. He said he was going to drive straight into a telegraph pole and kill us all. He didn't believe the baby was his, you see, even though it was. I wouldn't have minded him killing me, but not my baby.'

Reece's heart squeezed tight. Oh, dear God, he'd forgotten about the baby.

What was she going to do when she found out her baby *had* died? Because it must have. The Alanna he'd married had no child.

Which perhaps was why she wanted one. Quite obsessively.

The enigma that was the woman he'd married last year was finally coming clearer. Reece didn't have the entire picture yet, but lots of pieces were beginning to fall into place.

He watched with increasing concern as she bravely dashed the tears from her face, her mouth breaking into a travesty of a smile.

'The doctor says there's nothing wrong with me except a bump on my head. I can't believe how lucky I've been. I..'

She broke off abruptly, her eyes searching his.

'What is it?' she said. 'What's wrong?'

Reece didn't know what to say. The doctor had been right after all. He shouldn't have said anything. He was way out of his depth here.

She was staring at him, her eyes clearing from their earlier dullness to focus quite sharply on him. They travelled down over his clothes.. hardly the clothes of a policeman, he realized.. then back up to his face.

'You're not with the police, are you?' she said, her voice betraying bewilderment, and concern.

'No,' he confessed.

'Then who *are* you?'

'My name is Diamond. Reece Diamond.'

'Diamond,' she repeated. 'But that's the same name that the nurse called me.'

'That's right. *Mrs* Diamond.'

'But that doesn't make sense. I'm Mrs Malinowski, not Mrs Diamond.'

'You *were* Mrs Malinowski, Alanna. But you're not any more.'

'I…I don't get it.'

'You *were* in a car accident this morning. But it wasn't the accident you thought it was. You didn't jump out of the car on this occasion. A car hit us.'

'*Us?* You mean…you and me?'

'Yes.'

'But that isn't right. I've never been in a car with you. I don't even know you.'

God, but that hurt.

'I know you don't. Not at the moment. But you did and will again, in time,' he said, and hoped with all his heart that she would. 'You're suffering from a type of amnesia. That blow to your head seems to have temporarily eliminated a few years of your memory.'

Her eyes rounded like saucers on him.

'I know this has come as a shock to you, Alanna. I'm sorry there wasn't a gentler way to tell you. How old do you think you are?'

'I'm twenty-five,' she replied. 'Aren't I?' she added, suddenly looking very unsure.

'No, Alanna. You're thirty. And you're not Mrs Darko Malinowski any more. Like I told you, your first husband *is* dead, killed in a car accident some years ago.'

'My *first* husband?'

'Yes, you remarried. Last year. You're now Mrs Reece Diamond. That's who I am, Alanna. Your husband.'

She blinked, then just stared at him, her eyes still holding no recognition whatsoever, just one hell of a lot of shock. Plus total rejection of the idea.

Reece had had some low points in his life, but this had to count as one of the lowest.

What if she never remembers you? came the terrible thought. What if she doesn't like you the second time around? What if she wants a divorce?

'No,' she said, shaking her head in agitation. 'If Darko is dead.. and I suppose I have to believe you about that.. then I would never get married again. *Never!*'

The bitter certainty in her declaration told Reece that her marriage must have been sheer hell.

'I wouldn't,' she insisted fiercely. 'I *couldn't*. I..' She broke off, something even more appalling having catapulted into her head.

'My baby!' she burst out. 'What happened to my baby?'

Reece smothered a groan. He couldn't bear to be the bearer of such news. But there was no one else.

'I'm not sure, Alanna,' he said with a heavy sadness blanketing his heart. 'You've never mentioned a baby to me. Till we can check your medical records, or your memory returns, I have to assume you must have miscarried when you jumped out of that car.'

Her cry was the cry of a wounded animal. Loud and primal, her pain echoing through the room. It tore right through Reece, making him long to take her in his arms and comfort her. But when he reached for her, she reeled back from him, rolling over and curling up into a foetal ball, sobbing a tormented *no* over and over.

The nurse burst into the room, looking daggers at him before rushing to her patient's side.

'You were not supposed to upset her,' she bit out. 'I think you'd better leave.'

'You can think what you like,' he threw back at her. 'I'm her husband and I'm staying!'

'No, you're not,' a male voice pronounced as its owner strode through the open doorway.

He was possibly thirty-five, with a lean face, penetrating blue eyes and longish brown hair. He was wearing stonewashed jeans, a dark blue shirt and a black leather jacket.

'I'm Dr Beckham,' he said by way of introduction. 'The resident psych. Nurse, sit with the patient. You!' His finger stabbed towards Reece. 'You come with me.'

Reece's first reaction to such a brusque order was defiance. But then he remembered his desperate promise to God to be a better man.

It was still a somewhat disgruntled Reece who followed the psychiatrist out of the room. He'd barely reached the corridor before he whirled and stood his ground.

'I'm getting pretty sick and tired of doctors telling me I can't stay with my wife. Look, I'm not going home and that's final!'

A wry smile crossed the psychiatrist's face. 'Nice to see a husband who actually cares for his wife. You can go back to her after you've filled me in on exactly what's going on. Meanwhile, try not to worry. Dr Masur gave your wife a sedative earlier. She won't be able to hold out for too long before dropping off to sleep. Okay, now give!'

CHAPTER EIGHT

ALANNA'S return to consciousness was slow, her eye-lids fluttering up and down several times before they finally stayed open. Her brain was just as slow to register where she was. Even slower to remember what had brought her there.

'You've been in a car accident and lost your memory,' she told herself shakily, her hand coming up to feel the lump in her hair.

It was huge. And very sore to touch.

Yet, oddly, she didn't have a headache.

'Darko is dead,' she murmured, then shook her head in amazement.

But, dismayingly, so was her baby. Her precious, darling baby.

Five years ago it had happened, they said, but it was like yesterday to Alanna, the pain of loss very fresh and sharp. Tears threatened once more when suddenly, out of the corner of her eye, she glimpsed a pair of bejeaned legs.

'Oh,' she cried, her head whipping round to the right.

By the time Alanna realised that the man stretched out in the chair in the corner was fast asleep, she had her tears under control. Not so her quickened heartbeat.

Reece Diamond, he'd said his name was. Her husband. Her second husband.

No way, was her immediate reaction. No way!

Yet there was no reason for him to lie. No reason for him to still be here, if it wasn't true.

She stared at him again. He was incredibly handsome, with the type of chiselled features you saw on male models and movie stars. His hair was a sandy blond, wavy and worn slightly long at the front. His eyes, she recalled, had been blue, and strikingly beautiful. His body wasn't half bad, either. What she could see of it. Broad shoulders. Long legs. No visible flab.

Alanna could well understand lots of women falling for him. He was a sexy-looking man, as well as classically good-looking.

But not her.

After what she'd been through with Darko, Alanna knew she would never fall in love again. Or marry again.

Unless…

Her heart contracted fiercely. Was that the answer to this puzzle? Would she have married, just to have another baby?

Again, her reaction was negative. How could she have risked putting her life into the hands of another man? The notion was untenable. If she'd wanted a baby so much she would have found some other way. By artificial insemination. Or by asking a friend to be a sperm donor.

This last thought sent a bitter laugh bubbling up in her throat. A friend? She didn't have any friends.

At least she *hadn't* five years ago, when she'd been Mrs Darko Malinowski.

Alanna frowned, forcing herself to project ahead five years, trying to see what might have happened to her during that time interval.

Five years was a long time. Who knew what kind of person she had become after five years?

She tried to picture herself married to the man in the armchair. But whilst he was a very attractive man, her mind automatically baulked at the hurdle of actually sleeping with him. Yet she must, if she was his wife.

Did she enjoy it? she began to wonder as she gazed at him.

Her stomach flipped over at the thought. There'd been a time when she *had* enjoyed sex. But Darko had fixed that.

Had she somehow found pleasure again in a man's body?

Had she married for love, perhaps?

Again, Alanna refused to believe that could possibly be the case.

Darko had won her with love, the kind of love she'd never known a man could bestow upon a woman. But his love had been fool's gold and she had been the fool, mistaking his excessive attentions and constant gift-giving for genuine affection. She'd had no experience with that kind of sick obsession, so hadn't been able to recognise the warning signs. She'd thought his wanting to wait till their wedding night to make love for the first time had been incredibly romantic. She hadn't realised he'd be disgusted by her not being a virgin, or that he would feel threatened by her enjoying sex.

Their marriage had started to go horribly wrong long before their honeymoon had been over. But by then she'd felt trapped. Trapped by *her* love for *him*. Though of course it hadn't been love that had *kept* her tied to him. Eventually, it had been fear.

No, she decided bitterly. Love would not have made her marry this man.

So why had she become Mrs Reece Diamond?

The answer was a total mystery to her.

When she looked at him, nothing flickered in her brain. There were no flashes of *déjà vu*. Nothing.

'Reece,' she said, not to wake him, but simply to try out his name on her tongue.

He stirred immediately, his chin jerking up, his hands reaching to grab the arm rests of the chair as his eyes shot open and went straight to hers.

'Are you all right?' he asked anxiously, then seemed annoyed with himself. 'Stupid question. Of course, you're not all right. I'll go get the nurse.' He was on his feet in a flash and moving towards the door.

'No. No nurse!' she blurted out, stopping him mid-stride. 'Not yet,' she added more calmly.

'Are you sure?'

'Yes,' she said, surprising herself. Because she *was* sure.

Yet the twenty-five-year-old Alanna hadn't been

sure of anything. She'd been totally broken, with little will left of her own.

The alien decisiveness in her voice just now had to be the thirty-year-old Alanna talking, the one her brain couldn't consciously remember.

'Has any of your memory returned?' he asked rather anxiously.

'Unfortunately, no. But I *can* sense a difference in myself now that I'm calmer. I mean…I can see I'm not the same desperate creature who threw herself out of her husband's car five years ago.'

'That's good,' he said, nodding. 'Now, I really should go and call the doctor. He wanted to see you as soon as you came round.'

'What doctor are you talking about?'

'Dr Beckham. He's the resident psychiatrist here. Nice man. A neurologist has been called in as well to see about your memory loss. Dr Jenkins. But he has to drive back from the snowfields and won't be here for a while yet.'

Alanna gave a rueful shake of her head. 'A psychiatrist and a neurologist. I'm a right mess, aren't I?'

'You look pretty good to me,' he said. 'But then, you always do.'

Alanna blinked, startled by the compliment, plus her instant reaction to it. A warmth spread through her body, bringing a tingle to the surface of her skin and a faint flush to her cheeks.

Her brain might not remember Reece Diamond, but her body seemed to. There was a degree of relief and reassurance in her physical response to him. And a huge amount of curiosity.

'I have some things I have to ask you,' she said.

'Anything.'

'Could you please sit back down? You look like you're about to bolt.'

When he laughed, her eyes widened. Because she knew that laugh.

'You've remembered something, haven't you?' he immediately pounced.

'Yes. No. I don't know. Your laugh…'

'You often said you liked my laugh. And my sense of humour.'

Alanna mulled that statement over. After Darko, a sense of humour would certainly appeal to her. But it did not answer the most vital question in her mind. Till she got her memory back, only this man standing in front of her could do that.

'The thing I have to ask you,' she said tautly. 'It's very important. I simply must know.'

'What?'

'*Why* did we get married? I mean…I'm finding it hard to believe I ever got married again at all, but it seems that I did. The question still remains…*why* did I?'

He just stared at her, those beautiful blue eyes of his showing great reluctance to answer her.

'Please don't feel you have to say the supposed right thing, just because I've lost my memory. I don't want to be told lies. I'm not looking for empty words of love. God, no. That's the last thing I want you to tell me: that you love me. Darko spent our entire marriage telling me how much he loved me, then showing me how much he didn't. I want to know why we got married. It wasn't for love, was it?'

Reece raked his fingers through his hair, his frustration acute. What could he possibly say to her?

The truth again, he supposed. Yet the truth was not the truth any more. At least, not on his part. He *did* love her now. Hell, he loved her so much, his heart ached with it.

But she didn't want to hear that. She wanted to be told that their marriage had been made with their heads and not their hearts. Clearly, she was afraid of love. Did not trust it. Could not risk it again.

So he sat down on the side of the bed and told her the truth as it had been, up till today.

She listened, saying nothing, but frowning when he explained that their marriage had been a marriage of convenience, entered into for companionship and children. When Reece confessed he knew very little about her first marriage, not even her first husband's name, her face betrayed confusion.

'I must have said *something* to explain why I would enter a loveless marriage.'

'You led me to believe your first husband had been the love of your life and that you could never fall in love again after he died,' Reece explained. 'Since I'd had a similar experience, I didn't question your reason.'

'A similar experience?' she echoed, her eyes startled.

He told her about Kristine, though once again not revealing the events of their last day together. There really didn't seem any point at this stage. By the time he finished talking, a heaviness of spirit had taken hold of Reece. He found the true cause of Alanna's not wanting to be loved infinitely depressing. Because it meant her capacity for falling in love had been irreparably damaged. Even if she remembered him, her heart would never be his. He could see that now.

Suddenly, he couldn't take any more. He was tired, and his whole body was aching.

When he levered himself up onto his legs, he winced.

'You're hurt,' she said.

Reece found the concern in her voice frustrating in the extreme. He didn't want her concern. He wanted her love and her passion!

'I'm feeling a bit sore and sorry for myself,' he admitted brusquely. 'But nothing a hot bath and a few painkillers can't fix. Look, I really must go get the doctor now. Then I might go home. But I'll be back first thing in the morning.' Hopefully, by then, she might remember him.

'What about my mother?' she suddenly asked.

'What about your mother?' he returned, taken aback by the question.

'Is she still…alive?'

Now Reece was seriously taken aback. Alanna's mother was only fifty-one, unlike his own mother, who was in her late sixties. Why would Alanna think her mother might not be alive?

'Absolutely,' he said. 'Healthy as a horse. She's just become engaged to be married again.'

Her green eyes widened. 'You're kidding. Who to?'

'Bob. He's a maths teacher at Cessnock high school. They've been dating for some time.'

'Good Lord. This is unbelievable.'

'You were going to ring her tonight. Do you want me to do that for you, explain what's happened?'

'Are you saying we ring each other regularly, Mum and I?' Alanna asked with scepticism in her voice.

'All the time.'

'I'm finding this all a bit hard to take in.'

'I'll call her and get her to come down to Sydney.'

Panic filled her face. 'No, no, please don't do that. I don't want to see her just now. I...I need some more time by myself, to think, and to try to remember.'

'But she'll be hurt that you don't want her with you.'

'Will she?' Alanna said quite sharply. 'I doubt that.'

'You're living in the past, Alanna,' Reece said quite sternly. He really liked Judy and didn't want to see Alanna hurting her, however unintentionally. 'Whatever happened once between you and your mother has been smoothed over. You are very close now. She will want to be with you in this difficult time.'

Again, Alanna shook her head. 'I know what

you're saying is probably true. You have no reason to lie to me. But I just don't want to see her right now. I won't!' she said stubbornly.

Reece rolled his eyes. 'All right. I'll try to make her understand. Now, I really *have* to go get the doctor.'

'And then you definitely should go home,' came her unexpectedly solicitous advice. 'You look awfully tired.'

Reece couldn't help it. He smiled. 'That sounded like a wife talking.'

She smiled a small smile of her own. 'Yes, it did, didn't it?'

Their eyes connected, hers searching his with an anxious expression.

'Am I a good wife to you?' she asked, her voice heartbreakingly hopeful.

'The best,' he said, a lump having formed in his throat.

She shook her head. 'I find that hard to believe. Everything is so hard to believe.'

'Believe it,' he said, but through gritted teeth.

She stared at him for a long time before slowly nodding. 'I can see that it wouldn't be hard to be a good wife to a man like you. You're very patient. And very kind.'

Reece had to struggle not to laugh. Patient was the last thing he really was. As for being kind… People often called him kind and generous. But they were very superficial virtues when you were rich and successful. It was damned easy to throw your money around.

Reece momentarily toyed with the idea of making even more promises to God in exchange for Alanna's memory. If she went back to being the woman she'd been just before the accident, he could at least express his love for her in bed. And out.

That was better than nothing. But if she *never* remembered him, Reece feared he might never get to touch her again, let alone make love to her. He didn't yet know everything that bastard had done to her during their marriage, but he knew none of it had been nice.

Clearly, Mr Darko Malinowski had caused a lot of emotional damage to Alanna. Sexual damage as well. Reece understood now why she'd been the way she was during the early months of their married life. She'd been afraid to express herself sexually. Afraid of her true self, which was a very passionate and sensual woman.

Talking to a psychiatrist might do her the world of good.

'I'll go get Dr Beckham,' he pronounced firmly, and strode from the room.

CHAPTER NINE

'WHAT a lovely day it is,' Alanna said.

Lovely, weatherwise, Reece thought ruefully as he glanced across at his passenger. Not so lovely in other ways.

It was Wednesday morning, three days since the accident. He was taking Alanna home, and she still didn't remember a single moment of the last five years.

Physically, however, she was fine. The swelling on the side of her head had subsided. She had suffered some mild concussion, but a brain scan yesterday had shown no lasting damage.

Dr Jenkins..and Dr Beckham as well..had come to the conclusion that her memory loss was more of the psychological kind. The car accident had momentarily propelled her back to the previous car accident, a time of severe emotional and physical trauma. In defence, her brain had shut down her memory from that point in time, which was perverse in Reece's opinion. Far better if it had shut down her first twenty-five years, rather than the last five.

Both doctors believed her memory would return in time, especially once she was in her own home, surrounded by her own things.

Reece sure hoped so. Living with a wife who didn't

remember him wasn't going to be easy. He'd already decided to sleep in another room for a while, giving Alanna total space and privacy.

Reece now knew what her first husband had done to her. Alanna's mother had filled him in on the gross details when he'd rung her on the Sunday night.

Apparently, Darko Malinowski had been a refugee from abroad. An orphan, whose family had been massacred back in his home land, he had been an intense young man. Extremely good-looking in a tall, dark and handsome fashion. He'd been doing an engineering degree part-time at Sydney University and driving taxis to make ends meet when he'd met Alanna and fallen madly in love with her.

He'd pursued her avidly, showering her with little presents and poems, treating her like a princess. Alanna hadn't been able to resist such treatment, which was the total opposite of the way her own father had acted.

Judy had confessed to Reece that Alanna's father had been a pig of a man with no caring for his family at all. Alanna had never understood why she'd stayed with him. Judy's putting-up with such treatment had been the reason why mother and daughter had become estranged. They hadn't been reconciled till Darko had been killed and Alanna had gone home to Cessnock, a broken mess after miscarrying her baby. By then, she'd been much more understanding of why a woman stayed with a man she no longer loved and who treated her badly.

Judy had explained to Reece over the phone that

Darko had been a very possessive and jealous husband. He'd made Alanna's life a misery, questioning
her all the time over her movements, following her,
making scenes if Alanna wanted to go anywhere by
herself. When Alanna had tried to defy him one
Friday night, he'd tied her to a chair for the whole
weekend.

Reece had been appalled when he'd heard that,
more so when he thought of the time he'd suggested
bondage to Alanna. No wonder she'd shrunk back
from that idea. Reece vowed never to bring the subject up ever again. Or do anything that might remind
Alanna of her ghastly first husband.

'He was a mentally sick man,' Judy had said. 'But
physically very strong. Alanna told me she was ter-
rified of him. When she fell pregnant, she said she
hoped he'd be happy. But he wasn't. He accused her
of having an affair. He was convinced the baby be-
longed to some other man. When he threatened to kill
them all in the car, she knew he meant it. He always
carried through with his threats. So in a last-ditch at-
tempt to save her baby, she jumped out of the car.'

With this last thought in mind, Reece snuck a sidewards glance at Alanna and wondered if she was
afraid to be in a car. After all, this would feel to her
like the first time she'd been in a car since that orig-
inal accident.

He recalled how she'd hesitated to get into the
BMW this morning back at the hospital, claiming surprise that he drove such an expensive car. He swiftly
told her that this was a rented car, but his adding that

he usually drove a Mercedes had sent her eyebrows lifting once more.

Up till then, they hadn't talked about what he did for a living, or how much he earned, so he'd thought her surprise quite reasonable. He hadn't imagined for one moment that she might be afraid.

But she was sitting very still, he noted, with her hands clasped tightly in her lap. Her face was extra pale, but that could have been because she didn't have any make-up on. She was wearing the same jeans and cream jumper she'd been wearing last Sunday, though he'd brought her in fresh underwear. A matching pink bra and panties, which she'd frowned over… complaining that they were on the skimpy side.

Skimpy and sexy.

Reece scowled at himself when an image flashed into his mind of Alanna sitting there in nothing but that pink bra and panties.

Damn, but that was the last image of her he wanted in his head, especially now with no chance of their making love. He wouldn't even dare kiss her.

But the image stayed. And so did the desire that came with it.

Reece gave vent to a sigh. Life had turned very difficult indeed.

When Alanna heard the weary-sounding sigh she turned to look at Reece.

Poor man, she thought, being married to her.

But as her eyes moved over him Alanna realised her husband was anything but poor.

He was wearing a suit today, a superbly tailored grey single-breasted that shouted designer label. His business shirt was blue, which made his blue eyes look even bluer. His tie was gold. So was his wrist-watch. A gold Rolex.

Reece Diamond was no rough diamond. He drove expensive cars and dressed like a prince.

Clearly, she'd married money.

Was that the reason behind her marriage of convenience? she now wondered. Had she turned into a mercenary woman during the last five years?

As Mrs Darko Malinowski she'd never had much money. Darko had dropped out of university after their marriage. He'd claimed he could make more money driving cabs, but she suspected he'd spent most of his time following her. She'd secured a good job in a city hotel with her degree in leisure and hospitality, but within a year of their marriage Darko had been demanding she hand over her entire salary to him.

And poor frightened fool that she had been, she'd obeyed with only a token protest. Then, when he'd finally demanded she quit work to stay home and be a 'good' wife to him, she had. By then, she'd been close to having a nervous breakdown, anyway.

'We're nearly home,' Reece said, putting a halt to her trip down memory lane. What she had of her memory, that was.

'We live in Balmain?' she said, glancing at the street signs. At least she still knew Sydney and its suburbs.

'East Balmain,' he answered. 'On the water.'

One of the most exclusive areas west of the city.

Even before he turned into a wide paved driveway and stopped in front of a set of tall black security gates, Alanna knew their home would not be some ordinary little house, certainly nothing like the two-bedroom fibro cottage she'd lived in with Darko.

But as the gates swung slowly open she saw that her home was not a house at all, but a mansion. A huge white cement-rendered mansion with three garages on the side, a fancy fountain in the front yard and a double storey façade that screamed multimillionaire status.

'I didn't realise you were *this* rich,' she said.

'I haven't always been,' came his offhand reply. 'And I might not always be. The real-estate business is fickle.'

'You sell houses?' she asked as he drove through the gate, down a rather steep incline towards one of the garages, the door of which was automatically opening.

'I used to. I'm a property developer now. I buy land and build bigger buildings than houses these days. Mostly apartment blocks. But I've also dabbled in resorts and retirement villages.'

'You must have worked very hard to achieve so much at your age. I mean…you can't be all that old. You only look about thirty-five.'

'Close. I'm thirty-six, going on thirty-seven. And, yes, I have worked hard. Which reminds me, I have to go into the office today for a few hours. There are some urgent things which need my immediate attention. I hope you don't mind. I thought you might like some time by yourself, anyway. Of course, I'll show you through the house first. I do realise you won't remember where anything is.'

'No, don't do that,' she said swiftly. 'Dr Jenkins said to test myself wherever possible, see what I instinctively remember.'

'Do you remember your car?' Reece said, nodding towards the silver Lexus that they'd just drawn alongside.

She stared at the sleek, sporty-looking sedan and shook her head. 'No. I don't.'

'You keep the keys in the zippered side pocket of your handbag,' he told her. 'The one you have at your feet.'

She picked up the brown leather handbag..the very expensive brown leather handbag..and sure, enough, in the side pocket was a set of car keys, along with a natty little mobile phone. She'd already inspected the other contents of the bag back at the hospital so she knew she wore Pleasures perfume these days and had developed a penchant for mints. Her purse hadn't contained much cash, but she had one hell of a lot of cards, including two credit cards.

'Do I work outside the home?' she asked her husband.

His head turned to look at her. 'Do you feel that you do?'

'No. No, I don't think I do.'

'You had a good job in public relations at the

Regency Hotel when we met. But you resigned after we married.'

'So I'm an idle rich bitch,' she said, startling herself with her self-accusing tone. But, really, marrying for money was not, in Alanna's opinion, a nice reason to marry anyone.

'Absolutely not,' her husband said quite sharply. 'You're a career wife. And a darned good one.'

A career wife...

Alanna thought about that job description as she followed Reece through an internal entry door that opened into a wide hallway, leading down to an even wider foyer.

As she glanced around at the expanse of grey marble flooring Alanna supposed looking after a home like this *would* take some doing. The floor-cleaning job alone would be considerable.

But then she realised she would probably have a cleaner come in. Rich bitches always had cleaners.

'You didn't open any of the doors on your left as you passed,' Reece commented. 'What do you think was behind them?'

'I have absolutely no idea.'

'The servant's quarters. And the laundry.'

She stared at him. 'We have live-in servants?'

'Actually, no, we don't. You said you didn't want that. A woman does come in twice a week to do the heavy cleaning and the laundry. And you do occasionally hire a catering firm you like when we have a party. But only the large parties. You like to cook yourself for our smaller dinner parties.'

'Thank God I do something!'

'You do a lot, Alanna. I lead a very busy professional and social life. You are my right hand.'

Now she sounded more like his personal assistant than his wife. Alanna began to wonder if they *did* sleep together. Not that she was about to ask. Just the thought of sharing a bed with this man, this…*stranger*, disturbed her considerably.

Reece might be a very handsome man. But she still couldn't see herself enjoying sex with him. Or any man, ever again.

'Anything seem familiar to you at all?' he asked.

Alanna glanced around from where she was standing in the middle of the foyer. To her left and right were dual staircases leading upstairs to she knew not what. Bedrooms, she supposed. Straight ahead, a wide step separated the foyer from an enormous living area that opened out onto an equally huge terrace.

Beyond the terrace, on a slightly lower level, lay the most beautiful kidney-shaped swimming pool, complete with spa. Further on were lawns and gardens sloping down to the water. In the distance on the right was the harbour bridge. Straight ahead across the water lay the northern suburbs of Sydney, with lots of apartment blocks whose views would be almost as spectacular as this one.

Everything about this home was spectacular, from the marble floors underfoot to the Italian leather furniture to the magnificent artwork on the clean white walls. Hanging high over her head in the vaulted ceiling was a chandelier that would not have looked out of place in a palace.

But nothing felt familiar to her, least of all the man asking her the question. The only thing she remembered about him so far was his laugh.

And that might not have been a memory but a new attraction. She hadn't consciously been with a man who laughed in years.

'What do you think is down there?' Reece asked, pointing to the hallway that led off to the right beyond the staircase.

'Sorry. I simply have no idea.'

'My study, and the guest wing.'

'And what about these two doors over here?' he said, pointing to one on each side of the foyer, underneath the staircases.

'A powder room and a coat closet?' she tried.

'Close. They're both powder rooms, one for our male guests and one for the ladies.'

'Oh.'

I should have known, she thought ruefully. His and her toilets. I haven't just married money. I've married pots of money.

Suddenly, a wave of weariness washed through Alanna. Maybe it was physical, but she suspected it was more likely an emotional tiredness.

'Why don't you get back to work?' she suggested. 'I'll be fine here by myself.'

'Are you absolutely sure?'

'Yes. To tell the truth, I'm rather tired. I might have a lie down for a while. I...oh, no,' she groaned.

'What? What is it? Have you remembered something?'

'I forgot to bring home the lovely flowers you gave me in the hospital,' she said, genuinely disappointed at having left them behind. They'd been a huge basket of assorted flowers, with lots of Australian natives that would have lived on for quite some time.

He smiled softly at her. 'Don't worry. I'll get you some more.'

'Goodness, you don't have to do that.'

'Yes, I do. That's my job. To make my wife happy. As you have made me happy, Alanna,' he finished.

She stared at him. 'We're truly happy together?'

'Yes.'

'In bed, too?' she plucked up the courage to ask.

'In bed, too.'

Alanna swallowed. She found it impossible to get her head around the concept of ever finding pleasure in a man's body again.

But then she realised that this thinking was false. Five years had gone by since Darko had reduced her to a petrified wreck, incapable of feeling anything much but fear. Clearly, she'd emerged from that unnatural state to rediscover what she'd once been. A girl who, at the age of nineteen, had been shown the delights of the flesh by a man much older than herself. A girl who'd thrilled to the feel of her first orgasm. A girl who hadn't needed to be in love to enjoy being made love to.

Maybe she'd married Reece Diamond, not for his money, but for the most basic reason of all.

Sex.

Alanna recoiled at the idea. Really, that reason wasn't any more acceptable than marrying him for his money.

What if you married him for both those reasons? her merciless mind persisted. His money *and* his sex appeal. He sure has plenty of both.

'What on earth are you thinking?' he said, taking a step towards her, his eyes turning anxious.

Alanna blinked, then swallowed. 'I...I guess I'm still confused over why I went to that introduction agency you told me about. Becoming a career wife seems an unlikely choice for me. Given my first experience at marriage.'

'I see. Well, your mother might be able to help you with that. Why don't you give her a call?'

'No,' Alanna said immediately. 'I don't want to talk to my mother. Not yet.'

'Then perhaps you should have a talk with Natalie. Natalie Fairlane,' he added when she must have looked totally blank. 'The lady who runs the Wives Wanted introduction agency. Would you like me to call her for you and explain the situation? I'll see if she can pop in to see you tomorrow. Not today. I can see you're too tired for visitors today. You can ask her anything you want to know about who you were and what you wanted when you came to her. She would have done a very in-depth interview with you. Besides, talking to her might spark off something in your memory.'

'Yes. Yes, that would be a good idea,' Alanna said,

although not sure if she'd be pleased to discover what kind of woman she'd become. She seemed to be getting the picture of a very mercenary creature who'd gone into her second marriage for what she could get out of it. Reece might proclaim they were happy in bed together, but what if she was just pretending to enjoy sex with him, in exchange for living the life of Riley?

'I'll call her as soon as I get back to the office,' Reece offered kindly.

'Thank you.'

'My pleasure,' he said, and smiled one of those incredible smiles of his.

No wonder he was successful, with a smile like that. It made you want to do anything for him.

Anything but that, Alanna thought with a shudder.

It was no use. When she looked at her husband she saw a very attractive, very sexy-looking man. But she didn't want to go to bed with him. The thought he might expect her to share a bed with him tonight brought a stomach-churning panic.

'One thing before you go,' she blurted out.

'Yes?'

'About our sleeping arrangements,' she said, her face flushing with embarrassment. 'I mean...I...I don't want to...to...'

'It's all right, Alanna,' he said gently, his expression carrying both regret and understanding. 'I've already moved my things into another room. We'll wait till you get your memory back for that.'

'But...but what if I never get it back?'

His expression became quite steely, and stubborn. 'The doctors said you would remember everything in time.'

'But when? Tomorrow? Next year? In ten years' time?' She couldn't imagine a man like him waiting that long to have sex with his legal wife. Darko hadn't been able to go a day. He'd forced himself on her even when she'd objected, claiming there was no such thing as rape in marriage. A wife was her husband's possession. He could do with her as he willed, when he willed it.

'Soon,' Reece said optimistically. 'Now I have to go. Don't forget to eat something. There's lots of food in the kitchen.'

She had to smile. He really was a most considerate man. So different from Darko. Whatever her reasons for marrying Reece Diamond, she had chosen well.

'I'll be fine,' she said, and, without thinking, reached out to touch her husband lightly on his arm. 'You don't have to worry about me.'

He stared down at her hand, then up into her face. For a split second, she could have sworn she saw torment in his eyes. But then he smiled and patted the back of her hand.

'That's what you always say,' he said.

'Do I?'

'Yes. You are a very independent woman.'

'Am I really?' The concept amazed her.

'Trust me.'

Trust him…

Alanna didn't want to admit that she found it almost impossible to believe that she would ever trust another man.

Yet she must have. And, strangely, it felt right.

'I'm sorry,' she said as she withdrew her hand from his arm.

He frowned. 'Sorry for what?'

For forgetting you, she was tempted to say.

'For causing you so much trouble. It must be awkward having a wife who doesn't remember you.'

He laughed. Not an entirely happy sound. 'You could say that.'

'When do you think you'll be back today?'

He glanced at his watch. 'Mmm. It's already eleven. Probably not till six.'

'Do you want me to cook you dinner? I mean…is that what I normally do?'

'In the main. Though we do eat out quite a bit. Look, how about I bring something home with me? You do look tired. What would you like? Chinese? Thai? Italian?'

Her mouth pulled back into a wry smile. 'You tell me. What *do* I like these days?'

Again, something flickered across his eyes. Not torment this time. Something exciting. Something almost…wicked.

What *was* it he was thinking of that she liked?

Alanna swallowed. Surely not something sexual. Surely not *that*. Alanna had liked the taste of a man once, but it was difficult to like something when your husband forced you to do it, all the while twisting your hair and calling you a whore.

'I'll surprise you,' Reece said. 'If you need to ring me, my private number is the first one in the menu of your phone. The one in the bag you're holding. Now I have to go, Alanna.'

Reece stepped forward to take her shoulders and lightly brush his lips against her cheek. Only the briefest and most platonic of kisses, but it sent her heart racing in her chest. Goose-bumps broke out all over her skin.

'See you around six,' he added, and was gone, whirling on his heels and striding off the way they had come.

Her hand lifted to touch her cheek as she stared after him. One thing was certain. Her mind might not remember her husband, but her body was beginning to.

CHAPTER TEN

REECE's office was in the centre of the city, on the twelfth floor of a high-rise building that overlooked the harbour.

His suite of rooms was plush, but not overly large. Diamond Enterprises only had three permanent employees on staff. Reece himself. His personal assistant, Jake Wyatt, a gung-ho young tyro, and a female secretary/receptionist to front the reception desk.

Her name was Katie. She was thirty-eight years old, an ex-real-estate salesperson who'd wanted a change from the pressure of selling. She was blonde. Attractive. Diplomatic. Pragmatic. And best of all, happily married.

Reece liked to prevent personal problems at work.

'No calls for half an hour, Katie,' he announced as he swept through Reception shortly after eleven. 'And before you ask, no, Alanna hasn't got her memory back yet and, yes, I am not in the best of moods.'

'You don't want me to send out for your usual coffee and bagels, then?' she replied without batting an eyelid.

Bagels and coffee did sound good. He hadn't exactly been caring about eating lately and his stomach was beginning to rebel.

Reece stopped at the door of his office and threw

Katie a belated smile. 'You know how to tempt a man, don't you?'

She shrugged. 'Man cannot live by bread alone,' she quipped. 'But bagels are a different story.'

'You're right there. Get me two. And make the coffee strong. But not for twenty minutes. I simply must make a couple of calls first.'

'What about Jake?'

'What about Jake?' Reece repeated somewhat wearily. He wasn't sure if he could tolerate too much of Jake this morning.

'He wants to give you an update on that house-hunting job you gave him. You know…the one for your banker friend?'

'Ah, yes.' Before going on his honeymoon, Richard had given Reece the job of finding a suitable family home for himself and Holly, Reece promising to have several possibilities lined up for him to inspect by the time he came back.

But that wasn't for another four weeks. At this precise moment, he had other priorities.

'Look, tell Jake I'll talk to him about that some other time. Okay?'

'You're the boss.'

Reece forged on into his office, closing the door behind him and striding over to the highly polished, rosewood desk that had once graced an Englishman's residence, but which now sat sedately in front of a panoramic view of Sydney Harbour.

When Reece had leased this office eighteen months

earlier, he'd given considerable thought to the elegant décor, and the impressive view.

Today, he noticed neither. His thoughts were totally consumed with one subject and one subject only.

And it wasn't work.

Plonking down into the black leather swivel armchair, he snatched up his phone and selected Mike's number from his automatic dial menu. As much as he would prefer to be in a bar somewhere, drowning his sorrows, the time had come for him to follow through on the main promise he'd made to God last Sunday: to give financial assistance to the poor and underprivileged.

Maybe if he were extra generous, God might have more mercy and bring back Alanna's memory on top of saving her life. Because if she didn't ever remember him... If she decided she couldn't bear being married and wanted a divorce...

Both possibilities made Reece feel physically ill.

'Mike Stone,' Mike answered on the third ring.

'Mike, it's Reece.'

'Reece!' Mike sounded both surprised *and* wary. 'Look, mate, I hope you still haven't got your nose out of joint about last Saturday night. It wasn't *my* idea for Alanna to teach me to dance, you know.'

Reece had forgotten all about that. Last Saturday night seemed so long ago. Yet it had been less than four days.

'Yeah, I know, Mike. I'm not ringing about that.'

'Brother, I've never heard you sound so serious. I hope there's nothing wrong.'

As briefly as he could, Reece filled his friend in on what had happened to Alanna.

'Hell, Reece!' Mike protested after he finished his sad and sorry tale. 'Why didn't you tell me about this days ago? I might have been able to help. I could have at least taken you out for a drink or something. Got your mind off things for a while. You must have been worried sick.'

That was the understatement of the year!

At this point, Reece told Mike about the bargain he'd made with God.

'That's admirable, Reece,' Mike said. 'But...er... what has this got to do with me?'

'I thought I could do what you do. With poor kids. You know, buy them stuff they can't afford. Computers and sports gear. And pay for them to go on holidays. That kind of thing.'

'You mean that?'

'Sure I do. But I want you to decide how the money is spent. You'd know exactly where it's best needed and what to do with it.'

'How much money are we talking about here?'

'How about one million for starters? And one mil every year after that. Provided I'm still in the black. You know me, Mike. My finances go up and down like a flag on a flagpole.'

'I don't know what to say.'

'Just say thanks, mate. Then tell me where to send the money. I'll do it today.'

Two minutes later, Reece was off the phone, Mike's bank account number jotted down.

That was what he liked most about Mike. No bull. Just straight down to business.

He suspected his phone call to Natalie Fairlane would not be as brief.

Fortunately, he still had her number in his diary. Also fortunately, she answered. Reece knew that Natalie was the entire staff at Wives Wanted, which meant that when she was out of her office..her office being the downstairs front room in her Paddington terrace house..her secretary was her answering machine.

'Reece Diamond here, Natalie,' Reece said brusquely.

There was the smallest of hesitations at the other end before she replied.

'Reece! Hello. Don't tell me this is bad news and your marriage to Alanna isn't working out.'

'My marriage to Alanna has been working out fine,' he reassured her, surprised by her sentiments. He'd tabbed Natalie as an extremely pragmatic businesswoman, not anyone who would ever become personally involved in the marital matches she made.

Although a striking redhead with a knockout figure, she came across as cold and forbidding in the flesh. Yet just now, over the phone, she'd sounded quite warm, and genuinely concerned about his marriage.

'Then how can I help you?' Natalie asked, this time in a more puzzled tone.

He told her the situation with Alanna, pleased when she didn't interrupt him with a myriad silly questions.

Not that she was a woman who would ever ask

silly questions. Reece had never met a female quite like Natalie Fairlane. Highly intelligent, but one tough cookie!

He found it hard to imagine her ever getting married, despite her physical attractions. It would be a perverse man who found her daunting persona to his liking.

'How very distressing for you both,' she said when he'd finished his explanation. 'But for Alanna most of all. I had no idea that her first marriage had been bad. It's really rather odd. Women who have bad first marriages rarely back up for a second.'

'That's what's bothering Alanna the most,' Reece said. 'She can't believe she'd ever get married again. I was thinking you might be able to fill in that gap for her, but it seems you can't. Apparently, she didn't tell you the truth, either.'

'It seems so. But you know…I was always a bit worried about her.'

'Why was that?'

'I can't put my finger on it. Sometimes, I have an instinct for women who've been hurt. I sensed something in Alanna the moment I met her. But I mistakenly thought I had the answer when she told me that her first husband had been tragically killed. I should have gone with my gut feeling. I will, in future.'

Reece had a good idea at that moment why Natalie was as she was. At some stage in her life she'd been burnt by a man. Very badly.

'I wonder if you might still come and visit Alanna,' Reece asked. 'The doctors say she needs to be surrounded by people and things from the five years she's lost. You might spark some memory in her. It can't do any harm.'

'I'd be happy to,' Natalie replied crisply. 'When?'

'How about tomorrow? She's pretty tired today and still getting used to the house all over again.'

'Give me a time and I'll be there.'

'Shall we say ten in the morning?'

'Will you be there?'

Reece hesitated. He wanted to be with Alanna. Hell, he'd much prefer to be with her right now. But he wasn't stupid. He could see how stressed she was over the situation. He had to give her some space. Not hover over her. She'd had enough hovering from her first husband to last her a lifetime.

'No, I have to come in to work,' he said. 'I'm way behind. But the cleaner will be there. Her name is Jess. She'll let you in.'

Jess was a nice woman. She wasn't likely to upset Alanna. Or harass her with too many questions.

'Is the address the same as the one I have in my files?'

'Yes.' Reece had bought the house the day he'd decided to get married again. It had come totally furnished and decorated, the previous owner having moved overseas. 'Thanks a lot, Natalie. You'll have to let me take you out to lunch one day, as a thank-you.'

She laughed. 'Thanks, but no, thanks, Reece. I gave up having lunches with married men some years ago.'

Ah, so that was who had burnt her. A married man.

'I wasn't trying to come on to you,' he said. 'I love Alanna. Oh, damn,' he bit out immediately. 'For pity's sake, don't tell Alanna I love her. The last thing she wants is to hear that. Promise me you won't say anything.'

'All right. I promise. Poor Alanna,' Natalie went on with genuine sympathy in her voice. 'Once bitten that badly, for ever shy. And you're right. She wouldn't want to hear that you love her. Not with words. But that doesn't mean you can't show her how much you love her, Reece. I don't think that would be out of place.'

'Are you crazy?' he retorted. 'I daren't lay a finger on her at the moment.'

'Oh, dear.' Natalie's sigh carried exasperation. 'Do men always have to think in terms of sex? I wasn't talking about making love to her, Reece. I was referring to considerate little things you can do. Like taking her flowers…'

'I was already going to do that,' Reece said, though silently thanking Natalie for the reminder. He had a tendency to forget things when he was distracted. There was a florist in the foyer of this building. He'd dash down there shortly and buy some before that could happen. *And* send some to his mother.

'I have to go, Natalie,' Reece said when there was a soft tap tap on his office door. It would be Katie with the bagels and coffee. He knew her knock. 'I'll tell Alanna to expect you at ten. Thanks again. Bye.'

Reece glanced at his watch as he called out for Katie to come in. Twenty to twelve. He wondered what Alanna was doing.

Hopefully, getting her memory back.

CHAPTER ELEVEN

ALANNA was standing at the sink in the beautifully appointed white kitchen, washing up the mug she'd just used for coffee, when suddenly she sensed someone close behind her.

All the hairs on the back of her neck stood up, her mouth falling open as a scream bubbled up in her throat.

She whirled around, but no one was there.

She was alone.

Alanna leant back against the sink, her heart still racing.

Déjà vu?

But if that were the case, why didn't anything else in this house feel familiar? She'd had to search all the cupboards just now to find the wherewithal to make coffee. She hadn't been able to put her hand straight on a mug. Or the jar of instant coffee. Or the sugar.

None of the rooms downstairs had rung a bell in her brain. Neither had the outside. She'd wandered through the gardens for a while, staring at the pool and its surrounds before going down to the jetty and looking back at the house from that angle.

Nothing. Not a single flash of memory. Not even a flicker.

Shaking her head, Alanna decided that the time had come to go upstairs, to the master bedroom. She'd been putting it off. Why, she wasn't sure. Really, it was the one place where she would be most likely to remember something.

But, once again, she felt reluctant. And nervous.

Swallowing, she forced her legs to move, taking her from the kitchen back into the main living room, then up the wide marble step to the foyer. Once there, she delayed things a few minutes further by ducking into the ladies room.

The sight of herself in the vanity mirror brought her up with a jolt. She looked a fright.

'Lord, Alanna,' she said, pushing her hair back from her face. Okay, so she'd been blessed with wavy, naturally blonde hair that didn't need never-ending trips to the hairdresser to look good. It still could do with some love and attention. So could her face. Another good reason to go upstairs. She needed to shower, shampoo her hair and change her clothes. Her jeans and jumper felt grubby and her underwear was not on the comfortable side.

The bra was one of those underwired, half-cup contraptions that pushed her breasts up and together, her nipples in danger of popping out. The matching panties were terribly high-cut at the front, with just a thin strip of pink satin at the back.

Surely she owned some ordinary cotton underwear.

'Up those stairs you go, Alanna,' she lectured herself. 'And no more of this silly procrastinating.'

Emerging from the powder room, she turned and

walked more purposefully round to the right-hand side of the split staircase. As Alanna mounted the marble steps she passed by several large black and white pictures hanging on the white walls. Seascapes, they were. Very striking.

Had she chosen them? Or had they come with the house? They looked like something a professional decorator would have selected.

Actually, everything in the house looked like something a decorator would have chosen. Which meant what? She couldn't be bothered decorating her own home? Or was she happy these days to pay to have everything done for her?

Once again, Alanna felt weighed down by the amount of information she simply didn't know. It was extremely frustrating. Reece must be finding her memory loss frustrating as well.

Sighing, she continued up the curving staircase, which led to a rectangular-shaped landing. Straight ahead lay a pair of double doors with large silver knobs. In the centre of the wall on the left was a single door. Another door centred the wall on the right.

Logic told Alanna that the bedroom she'd shared with her husband lay behind the double doors straight ahead. But, once again, she checked the other rooms first.

Both were bedrooms. Both had *ensuite* bathrooms. The last one Alanna looked into..decorated in blue and white..had been slept in recently. The bedding was askew and there were some clothes hanging on the back of a chair. A black leather jacket. And a pair of stonewashed jeans.

Clearly, this was where Reece was sleeping at the moment.

His consideration for her was touching, but rather amazing. She wasn't used to her feelings being considered.

By the time Alanna pushed open the double doors, she was very curious to see what kind of room they shared, especially what kind of bed.

It was simply huge. A four-poster, but not an antique. The frame was painted white, which was proving to be the main colour throughout the whole house. The quilt was luxury itself, made in white satin, and padded, the squares sewn with a silver thread.

Considering the size of the room, there wasn't a lot of furniture in it. Two white bedside chests. Two white cane chairs and a white dressing table, showing an array of cosmetics and perfume that would have cost a small fortune.

Alanna walked over to the dressing table and pulled open the top two drawers, her eyes widening at the contents. She'd never seen so many matching sets of bras and panties.

All echoed the style of the pink satin set she had on today. Half-cup bras and G-string panties.

The second set of drawers was devoted to other sexy garments. Silk pyjamas, lacy teddies and satin corselettes, as well as stay-up stockings with lacy tops.

It seemed that the Alanna who'd married Reece Diamond wasn't into cotton underwear.

Clearly, her second husband liked his wife to look sexy, an observation that should have already been obvious to her by the pictures on the bedrooms walls.

She'd been avoiding looking at them. Black crayon drawings on white paper, they were, with silver frames. The subjects were all women in various states of undress. None was an actual nude but all were exotic and highly erotic.

Now *these*, Alanna felt sure she hadn't chosen.

Yet, there again, how *could* she be sure?

She shook her head again. Losing chunks of your memory was a dreadful thing, Alanna decided as she moved on into the biggest and most luxurious *en suite* bathroom she had ever seen.

Floor-to-ceiling marble. Silver fittings. His and her vanities, not to mention a spa bath, toilet and bidet.

The long mirror above the vanities slid back, Alanna soon discovered, revealing shelves full of an array of medicines and toiletries.

She frowned as she picked up a packet of sleeping tablets prescribed to her. Did she have trouble sleeping? Wasn't she happy as Mrs Reece Diamond?

Reece had said they were happy, but maybe he was lying.

But why would he lie?

If they weren't happy, he had the best excuse possible now to get rid of her. Yet all he'd been since the accident was kind and considerate and caring.

It crossed Alanna's mind that maybe he didn't know she was unhappy.

Alanna sighed. She was sick and tired of speculating. Aside from being frustrating, it was emotionally exhausting.

Sliding the mirrored door back into place, she turned to glance one last time around the bathroom, but nothing sparked any memory in her. Not the packet of sleeping tablets. Or the large corner spa bath. Or the shower recess. Or the...

Alanna's eyes whipped back to stare at the shower recess.

Built for two, it had twin shower heads, along with his and hers shelves, filled with personal hygiene products. Shampoos. Conditioners. Shower gels.

Her mouth dried as she tried to imagine having a shower in there with her husband.

Did they do that? Did they wash each other's backs, and other places? Did she let him do other things to her in there? Was that what he'd been thinking of when he'd smiled over what she liked?

Alanna could not imagine liking anything of a sexual nature ever again.

Yet her heart was racing.

Was it fear of such intimacies making it do that? Or a subconscious excitement?

Annoyed with herself for continuing with these useless speculations, Alanna spun on her heel and marched from the room, telling herself not to be such a masochist.

One step at a time, Alanna, the doctor had said to her. Don't try to hurry things. Don't stress.

All she had to do today was reacquaint herself with this house, and her personal belongings. Which she was in the process of doing.

One last door in the bedroom called to her. It led into a walk-in wardrobe, again of the his and her variety, and very spacious.

On the right side were rows of neatly arranged suits, shirts, trousers and jackets—all expensive looking—confirming the opinion Alanna had already formed that her husband was a snappy dresser.

The left side was devoted to women's clothes.

Her clothes, Alanna had to tell herself as she stared at the many racks.

The first thing that struck her was the lack of bright colours. That *had* to be a hangover from her marriage to Darko, who'd hated her wearing anything that brought attention to her.

But as her eyes began to scan the huge array of outfits in closer detail Alanna soon realised that she dressed very differently as Mrs Reece Diamond from when she'd been Darko's wife.

Her evening clothes had her eyes almost popping out of her head. One gown in particular brought a shocked gasp to her lips. It was a long slinky number in champagne-coloured satin.

The front was daring enough with its low-cut neckline and unlined bodice. The back was beyond daring. Because there was no back. Nothing down to the waist. And further!

No way could you wear any underwear at all under that dress. Everything would show, even the tiniest G-string.

Alanna tried to get her head around her wearing such a dress in public. Darko would have killed her rather than let her wear something like that!

Shuddering, Alanna shoved the dress back along the rack and looked at the next dress. It was made in white satin and wasn't much better.

Suddenly, she spotted something in red peeking out at the far end of the rack of evening dresses.

Oh, no, she thought despairingly. A scarlet dress to go with her new scarlet soul!

But when she pulled the red dress out, Alanna was relieved to see that it wasn't a case of more of the same. The red dress was bright in colour, but quite modest in style.

When she checked the rest of her wardrobe, however, any relief reverted back to agitation. Nothing was quite as revealing as the first dress she'd looked at. But a lot of her going-out clothes were still very sexy. Short, tight skirts and figure-hugging jackets. Slinky-looking trousers and a range of low-cut tops made in sensual materials. Silk. Satin. Even see-through. Her shoes were show-stoppers as well, strappy and sexy, with high, high heels.

To say Alanna was stunned was an understatement. Wearing such clothes was as unbelievable to her as remarrying and enjoying sex. What kind of woman had she become?

Fortunately, her casual wardrobe wasn't of the

same ilk, consisting of track suits, jeans, shorts and an assortment of T-shirts, pastel coloured blouses and lightweight jumpers.

At least she wouldn't have to greet Reece tonight dressed like some tart. Or a tease.

Although perhaps that was what he liked.

Another shudder ran through her. This was all too alien. Too different. Too stressful.

One moment, she'd been an abused doormat of a wife who hardly dared step outside her front door. The next she was some property tycoon's trophy wife who dressed to kill, and to thrill.

Who could blame her if her overriding emotion at this moment was confusion? Alanna didn't know whether to scream, or to cry.

Shaking her head, she grabbed some casual clothes—a navy track suit and white T-shirt—and was heading back to the bathroom when the phone sitting on the nearest bedside chest began to ring.

The sound brought her to a shaky halt, her eyes darting nervously over at the darned thing. She didn't want to answer it. What if it was someone she should know but didn't?

But what if it's Reece?

She *had* to answer it. He'd worry if she didn't.

Tossing the clothes onto a chair, she hurried over to pick up the phone.

'Hello?'

'Alanna? Is that you?'

Alanna cringed. Her worst fear had just material-ised. She had no idea whom she was speaking to, except that it was a woman with a rather posh voice. Sinking down on the side of the bed, she clutched the phone to her ear and prayed for inspiration.

'Er…yes, it's me.' No way did she want to launch into some lengthy explanation about the accident and her loss of memory. If she could bluff her way through this call, she was going to.

'You sound odd. Are you ill?'

'I was lying down,' she invented. 'I have a migraine.'

'You poor thing. You get those a lot, don't you?'

Did she?

'At least that explains why you weren't at the gym today,' the woman rattled on. 'I knew something had to be wrong for you not to show up two days in a row. I presume you won't be coming out with us tonight as well. The girls are going to be *so* disappointed.'

Alanna blinked. So she went to the gym quite a bit, did she? And had nights out with the girls. Maybe she *was* happy.

Pity she didn't know whom she was talking to. But Reece would probably know. She'd ask him tonight.

'I don't think I should,' she said. 'Sorry.'

'Oh, darn. Our nights out are never the same without you, darls. You're such fun to be with. Oh, well. Next time. I hope you feel better soon. Bye.'

'Bye…'

Alanna hung up, feeling even more amazed, and confused. Not only did she dress sexily these days, she was an exercise junkie and a life-of-the-party extrovert.

Yet she was nothing like that at all!

Suddenly, it was all too much for Alanna. Tears of utter frustration filled her eyes. She wanted her memory back. Not tomorrow. Or next week. Or next month. She wanted it back today, this afternoon, *before* Reece came home tonight. She wanted to be able to greet him at the door and say, 'Hello, honey. I'm so glad you're home. I remember you now, and yes, you were right. We *are* happy. And, yes, I am a good wife.'

But Alanna was afraid that might not be the case. Afraid that she might have gone into this marriage out of some kind of sick revenge.

Please God, don't let me have become a cold-blooded bitch, she prayed as the tears spilled over and streamed down her face. Or a mercenary cow. Or, worse still, a heartless whore!

CHAPTER TWELVE

REECE had been watching Alanna toy with her Thai beef satay for quite some time before he decided he could no longer ignore her mood. When he'd first arrived home, she'd seemed happy and appreciative of the flowers he'd brought her, as well as the wine and the food, but now she looked distracted and her appetite was zero.

'Is there anything wrong, Alanna?' he asked quietly.

They were sitting on either side of the breakfast bar on stools, Alanna having refused to eat in the formal dining room.

'No, no,' she said, glancing up at him. 'The food's delicious. I'm just not very hungry.'

'It's your favourite,' he said.

'Is it?' she said rather listlessly, and moved her meal slowly round the plate again.

Reece wasn't sure what to do. He could understand her feeling down. It must be dreadful, losing five years of your life, especially when you found yourself back in a part of your life that was awful.

In the end, he decided not to press.

'More wine?' he said, scooping the bottle out of the ice bucket and refilling her glass. 'This is your favourite, too,' he added. 'You simply adore New Zealand whites.'

Alanna picked up her glass and took a sip, her expression appreciative, then thoughtful.

'Do I drink much?'

Her question surprised him. So did the sudden edge he heard in her voice.

'You like your wine,' came his careful reply. 'But I've never seen you drunk. No, I take that back, you did get seriously sloshed one night.'

'What night was that?'

'Our wedding night.'

'Oh,' she said, and a fierce blush scorched her cheeks.

'We didn't sleep together before we were married,' he explained. 'You didn't want to. Knowing what I know now,' he added gently, 'I imagine you might have been nervous.' And then some. Judy had told him when they'd been discussing Alanna just last night that, before her marriage to him, she hadn't been to bed with a man since the dreaded Darko.

Her eyes searched his, curiosity finally overriding any embarrassment. 'What was it like...our first night together?'

'It was fine.'

His answer seemed to trouble her. But there was little point in giving the event glowing compliments when she'd hopefully recall the event herself one day.

To be bluntly honest, he'd had to work very hard to get her to relax. Her first orgasm had taken him an hour, plus every ounce of lovemaking skill he had. Then, afterwards she'd passed out like a light.

'That doesn't sound too good,' she said.

'It got better.'

She frowned at him. 'How much better?'

'A lot better. Look, Alanna, let's talk about something else,' Reece said sharply, his body having automatically responded to thinking of her and sex in the same breath.

Alanna's back stiffened at his curt tone.

'God, I'm sorry,' Reece immediately apologised. 'I didn't mean to snap to you like that. It's just…damn it all, there are no excuses. I'm sorry.'

'No, no,' she said swiftly. 'Tell me. I want to know what I did that annoyed you.'

'What *you* did? You didn't do anything. It's me.'

'What about you?'

He looked at her and shook his head. 'You don't want to know.'

'But I do. You've been so kind. Bringing me those flowers,' she said, nodding towards where they were sitting down the other end of the breakfast bar, an elegant display of multicoloured flowers in a basket. 'Not to mention this lovely food and wine. I've never known a man quite like you. No, that's not altogether true. You do have some of the attributes of a man I knew once.'

'Not Darko, I hope.'

'Lord, no!'

'Who, then?'

She smiled a rather shamefaced smile. 'He was my tutor at university.'

'And?' Reece prompted.

'He was my first lover. I was nineteen. He was forty.'

'Ah. The experienced older man.'

'Very,' she said, and blushed once more.

Reece now knew where she'd learned some of the tricks she'd shown him last Saturday night.

Damn. They were back to sex again. He was never going to get to sleep tonight. Best change the subject.

'By the way, I rang Natalie Fairlaine today,' he said. 'The lady from Wives Wanted? She's going to drop in tomorrow morning around ten. I've explained the situation so you won't have to go into that. It's the cleaner's day tomorrow, too, by the way. Her name's Jess.'

Alanna looked unhappy at this news. 'I don't mind about this Natalie woman coming. But does the cleaner have to come? I'm more than happy to do the cleaning till I get my memory back. Please put her off, Reece. Please.'

Reece sighed. 'Very well. I'll cancel the cleaner. But only until you get your memory back.' He supposed it was better she kept busy, rather than just mope around.

'Thank you. I simply hate the thought of having to deal with people who seem like perfect strangers to me. Some woman rang me today and it was so awkward.'

'You never mentioned that. Who was it?'

'I have no idea. Someone I go to the gym with. She had a posh voice.'

'Ah, that would be Lydia. There's quite a group of you who go to the local gym together. You go out with them on a Wednesday night as well. I should have warned you. I forgot. I suppose she was calling about that.'

'Yes, she was.'

'What did you tell her?'

'Nothing. I was able to bluff my way out of the situation by saying I had a migraine. The funny thing is, she said I get lots of those.'

'I wouldn't say lots. But you do get them occasionally.'

'I see... So, is this Lydia my best friend?'

'No. You don't really have a *best* friend. Although you've become quite close to Holly over the last few weeks.'

'Holly,' Alanna repeated, frowning. 'No, that name means nothing to me, either. Who's Holly?'

Reece explained about Holly and the wedding last Saturday, and how Holly and Richard would be away on their honeymoon for the next month.

'I have to say you looked absolutely gorgeous in your red bridesmaid dress,' he said, then wished he hadn't, the compliment taking his mind right back to Saturday night.

'Oh!' she exclaimed. 'I saw that dress today when I was going through my clothes. So that's why it was so different from all my other dresses. It was a bridesmaid dress!'

'Not quite your usual taste,' Reece said. 'But it suited you.'

'Yes, I…er…I noticed what my usual taste was,' she said. 'I dress rather provocatively, don't I?'

'I *like* the way you dress.'

'Darko would have ripped most of those clothes off me,' she said.

'Well, I'm not Darko,' he ground out, feeling angry for her. And sad at the same time.

'No,' she replied, her eyes searching his face. 'You certainly aren't…'

Reece found himself gripping his fork as if he were a drowning man holding onto a scrap of wreckage. The way she was looking at him. Not with love, or mindless desire. But with the most ego-stroking admiration, and heart-rending gratitude.

He'd never wanted to kiss her so badly. Just kiss her, and hold her. Comfort and reassure her.

His love for her expanded from his heart outwards in ever-increasing circles till it filled every pore in his body.

'I would never hurt you, Alanna,' he said with a fierce tenderness. 'Never.'

Suddenly, tears filled her eyes.

'I just wish I could remember you,' she choked out.

'You will. In time.'

'How can you say that?' she cried, dashing the tears away with her hands. 'I might never get my memory back. Doctors don't know everything. They could be wrong.'

Reece could well understand her feelings of distress

and panic. It would be easy to surrender to panic himself. But they couldn't both start falling apart. Alanna needed him to be strong for her.

'We'll cross that bridge when we come to it,' he said firmly. 'Meanwhile, you're not frightened of me, are you?'

'No…'

Damn. She could have sounded a bit surer. He'd done everything he could not to alarm her.

'Then everything will be all right. Trust me.'

'Trusting a man doesn't come easily to me, Reece.'

'I can imagine. But you *have* learned to trust again, Alanna. Otherwise, why would you have married me?'

'I suppose you're right,' she said with a frown.

'Talk to Natalie tomorrow,' Reece said. 'She'll tell you the kind of woman you were when you went to her agency, searching for a husband.'

'That's what worries me.'

'What do you mean?'

'I'm not sure I'll like that Alanna.'

'I don't see why not.'

Her face carried agitation. 'She's nothing like me.'

'In what way? Give me any example.'

'The clothes I wear, for starters. There's this one particular dress in my wardrobe. An evening gown. I mean, all my clothes are rather sexy, but this one is positively indecent!'

'Ah yes, I know the one you mean. It's made of satin. In a pale fawn colour.'

'Yes, that's the one. I can't imagine ever buying a dress like that, Reece, let alone wearing one.'

'You wore it all right. But only the once. And you didn't buy it. *I* did.'

She stared at him.

'It was a bit over-the-top, I admit,' he said ruefully. 'But you have the body to carry it off.'

'But I couldn't have worn any underwear with a dress like that!' Alanna protested, her tone horrified.

'True.' Not a good reminder. Reece recalled being turned on to the max during that party. He was turned on now, just thinking about it.

'And that didn't bother me?' she questioned him, her expression sceptical.

'Maybe a little. You told me later that night that you wouldn't be wearing it again till you had the straps shortened.'

'I doubt that would make much difference. It would still be a slut's dress.'

Reece came close to dropping his fork. So *this* was what was bothering her. She equated sexy clothes with being immoral.

That was certainly not *his* Alanna's way of thinking. She believed a woman had the right to wear whatever she liked.

The Alanna of five years ago, however, must have been brainwashed into a far more prudish frame of mind.

That appalling Darko had a lot to answer for!

But even as Reece blamed Darko for Alanna's present qualms he struggled to put aside his own guilt over why he'd chose such a dress for his wife. He was also pretty sure he wouldn't be letting her wear that satin number again.

Still, that wasn't the point at the moment. The point was to reassure Alanna over the woman she'd become.

'Alanna, you are in no way a slut,' Reece said firmly. 'In the last five years, women's fashion has become increasingly glamorous and sexy. You are not the only woman wearing such dresses. It's quite acceptable to dress provocatively for a party, especially when the wearer has a body as slender and beautiful as yours.'

She flushed again. 'Darko always said I was too skinny.'

The bastard. Reece's teeth clenched down hard in his jaw.

'You're perfect in every way,' he insisted, perhaps a little too passionately.

Reece decided to change the subject once more. Get right away from Alanna's perfect body.

'If you're not going to eat any more of that,' he said, 'why don't I get rid of it and make us both some coffee?'

Her eyes showed surprise. '*I* should be getting the coffee. You've been at work all day.'

'Do you think you can manage? I mean…you might not know where everything is yet.'

'I know where the coffee is,' she said rather drily. 'That's the first thing I looked for.'

He laughed. 'You're not too good without your coffee.'

'That's another thing which is strange. I never used to like coffee at all. Now I can't seem to get enough.'

'Our tastes change as we get older,' Reece said carefully.

'I suppose so. But I still find it hard to believe how much I've changed in five years. I can't recognise myself at all.'

'Try not to think about things too much, Alanna,' Reece advised her. 'Try to relax.'

'Relax! How can I possibly relax?' she threw at him in a burst of frustration. 'Or not think about things! My mind doesn't stop. It just goes round and round. I don't know who I am any more!'

'You're Alanna Diamond,' Reece said as he slipped off the stool and stood up. 'My wife.'

His wife.

Alanna swallowed, her gaze dropping away from his handsome face as those feelings swamped her again, feelings that made her face grow hot and her skin tingle all over.

The moment he'd walked in the door tonight, carrying those lovely flowers, she'd felt different with him. More aware of herself as a woman. And as his wife.

Whenever she looked at his mouth, she thought of him kissing her. Whenever she looked at his hands she thought of them touching her. Whenever she didn't look at him at all..such as now..her mind flooded with far more explicit images, images that made her mouth dry and her heart race, images that she hoped were memories, and not fantasies.

Alanna's head spun with the intensity of her desire, every muscle in her body stretched tight as a drum.

Try to relax, he'd said.

No way was she ever going to relax whilst in his presence. She had to find some excuse to leave him. To be alone.

'I...I seem to be coming down with a headache for real,' she said, and finally looked up at him again.

His frown carried concern. 'I hope it's not a migraine.'

'I hope not as well. Is there anything special I take when I get one?'

'I'll get them for you,' he replied, walking over to open a built-in cupboard high above the fridge.

When he reached up to rifle through the contents, his blue business shirt stretched tight across his shoulder muscles. Alanna found herself staring at him and wondering if he looked as good naked as he did in clothes.

By the time he turned back round with a packet of pills in his hand, she hoped she wasn't blushing again.

'You usually take a couple of these,' he said, putting them down on the granite benchtop next to her. 'Then you lie down in a darkened room and try to sleep it off. Sometimes, you take a sleeping tablet as well. There's a packet in the cabinet in the bathroom.'

'Yes, I saw them and wondered what they were for. Would you mind if I skip the coffee and just go do that?' she said, hoping she didn't look as guilty as she felt.

He shrugged his broad shoulders. 'Why should I mind? I'm just sorry you have a headache on top of everything else.

'No, I'll do that,' he said sharply when she stood up and started clearing away the plates. 'You just go and look after yourself. But why don't you try a relaxing bath before you start popping pills? It might be a tension headache more than a real migraine.'

Alanna found a polite smile to hide her shame. 'Yes, I'll do that. And thanks again, Reece. For everything.'

'My pleasure,' he said, then did the worst thing he possibly could do to her. He smiled.

And there they were again. Those feelings. And those mental images.

With a strained smile, Alanna snatched up the painkillers and hurried from the kitchen, increasing her pace across the living-room floor, hardly drawing breath till she was safely out of Reece's sight and climbing the staircase.

By the time she reached the master bedroom, her lie was fast becoming a reality, wavy-edged circles dancing in front of her eyes.

Punishment, Alanna decided, for being a liar *and* a slut.

Groaning, she dashed into the bathroom and took a couple of the painkillers, post-haste. Then, because it was still so early, she ran herself a bath, adding some of the bubble bath and bath salts and turning on the spa jets.

Half an hour later, she emerged from the triangular-shaped bath, her body all perfumed and pink, but still with the most dreadful headache. In desperation, she popped a couple of the sleeping pills and went in search of something to wear to bed.

But all of the sexy negligee sets in the walk-in wardrobe screamed slut to her. So she went to the dressing table and pulled out the set of pink silk pyjamas she'd seen there earlier in the day. They were less outrageous, though still very sensuous to wear and the silk felt cool against her water-warmed skin.

Her headache had intensified by the time she crawled into the huge four-poster bed, but her mind was definitely becoming fuzzy. Those sleeping tablets were finally working, thank God. She desperately needed some respite from the pain in her head and the confusion in her mind. She needed to feel nothing but peace. Or, better still, nothing at all.

Fifteen minutes later, Alanna's wish seemed to be granted as with a small sigh she slipped off to sleep.

But there was no escape from emotional torment, even in sleep. Dark dreams awaited Alanna in the night, dreams of danger and Darko, of hurt and horrors, of love betrayed and trust destroyed.

CHAPTER THIRTEEN

REECE was in bed, reading a book, trying to make himself tired enough to sleep, when he heard the scream.

'Alanna!'

Jumping up, he dashed for the master bedroom, turning on the overhead light as he burst through the door and raced over to the bed.

She was curled up in a ball in the middle of the bed, her eyes squeezed tightly shut, her head bent almost to her chest.

'No, please, Darko,' she whimpered. 'Please…'

Reece's heart almost broke to see her like that. It was one thing to hear Alanna's mother tell him about what that monster had put Alanna through. Another to hear for himself how frightened she had been.

The poor darling. No wonder she suffered from migraines.

He had to wake her. Bring her back from the horrors of her past. Make her see again that Darko was dead and she was safe. With him.

'Alanna,' he said as he shook her gently by the shoulders.

Her eyes flew open, terror still in their green depths.

'It's me,' he said swiftly. 'Reece. Your husband. Remember?'

'Reece. Oh, Reece!' she sobbed, her hands coming up to cover her face, her shoulders shaking uncontrollably as she began to weep.

Reece's heart filled to overflowing with love, and the need to show that love. Not sexually. Just physically.

'It's all right, darling.' Without a moment's hesitation he lifted the bedclothes and slid in beside her. 'You're safe,' he said, and wrapped his arms tightly around her.

For a split second, she stiffened, but then she sank against him, still weeping, but not quite so hysterically.

'Reece,' she choked out once more, and wound her arms around his back. 'Not Darko.'

'No, not Darko. I'm nothing like Darko. Hush, my darling,' he murmured as he stroked her hair. 'Hush.'

How long did he hold her like that, soothing her, stroking her, making her feel safe? It might have been fifteen minutes. Maybe longer. He couldn't be sure.

Neither was he sure of the moment when his soothing started to change to seducing.

Desire for her had snuck up on him. Slowly. Seditiously. Before he knew it, he was fiercely erect and he was kissing her mouth, softly at first, then with more purpose, and passion.

For a few moments, her mouth froze under his, but then it relaxed and melted and turned to liquid heat, Reece's mind blazing with male triumph at the speed of her surrender. She might not remember him consciously, but her body did. It was telling him so in no uncertain terms, her tongue as avid as his as they entwined with each other.

She moaned softly when he withdrew.

He levered himself up on one elbow and looked down into her flushed face.

'Alanna, I want to do more than kiss you,' his conscience compelled him to say. 'Tell me now if you don't want me to continue.'

She said nothing. Just stared up at him.

Reece smothered a groan, his gaze dropping to where her nipples were outlined like little rocks against her pink silk pyjamas. Yes, her body wanted him. But what about her mind? Could he even say she was in her right mind at this moment? Wasn't he taking advantage of her need for someone.. possibly anyone.. to comfort her?

Man and woman had been using sex as an instrument of comfort since Adam and Eve.

'Say something,' he insisted, his voice raw with his own need.

He would stop if she wanted him to. He loved her too much to risk causing her any hurt, either emotional or physical.

'Yes,' she said, her voice low and quivering.

Yes? Yes, what?

Reece groaned. 'You want me to stop?'

'No!'

No.

His loins leapt at the news. She didn't want him to stop.

Never had a woman admitting she wanted him meant so much to Reece.

'Oh, Alanna,' he whispered, his right hand trembling as it stroked down her lovely face.

He almost said he loved her then. Almost. But, luckily, he bit his tongue in time, bending his mouth to hers instead.

With her permission, the urgency of his own need had lessened. Giving Alanna pleasure was what he wanted most. Making her *feel* loved without his having to say it.

Natalie was right about men. They did prefer to express their love physically.

But sometimes that was the best way for them. Most men weren't wonderful at words, or sentimental gestures. Besides, that type of thing could just be a cover for lies, or con-jobs. When a man made love to a woman, his real feelings for her came through in his actions.

Reece had quite recently thought his feelings for Alanna were mainly lust. But that was certainly not true any more. He didn't want any kinky positions tonight. Or for her to do *anything*. Just to let him love her.

His head lifted again, leaving her eyes clinging to his in the most heart-stopping way. He watched her face as his hands went to the small pearl buttons on her pajama top, alert for any sign of protest, or returning panic.

But all she did was take a deep breath.

His fingers fumbled a little on the last button, his own breath becoming suspended as he bared her chest to his eyes.

It was almost as if he were seeing her body for the first time. *Feeling* it for the first time.

When his right hand brushed lightly over the tips of her breasts, she sucked in sharply. Reece glanced up to make sure it was all right for him to go on.

Her eyes were big on him, her lips apart, her breathing shallow and quick.

Encouraged, he bent his mouth to her right nipple, licking it gently with his tongue.

She gasped, her back arching.

He looked up again. This time, her eyes were tightly shut but her lips had fallen even further apart.

Taking this as a good sign, he resumed his attentions on her breasts, moving his mouth from one nipple to the other, licking them softly, then sucking them oh, so gently.

Her moans of pleasure thrilled him. And aroused him. Reece began finding it harder to be gentle, and patient.

But gentle and patient he remained.

It was she who became impatient, surprising him when her hands reached to push down on the elastic waistband of the satin boxer shorts he was wearing, then at the bottom half of her own pyjamas.

Reece was only too happy to comply with her wishes by then, stripping himself, then her in double-quick time.

'Are you sure, Alanna?' he asked her one last time before his control totally deserted him.

'Yes,' she said, and reached for him.

They both gasped as they came together, Reece stunned by the emotion that welled up in him as his flesh filled hers.

He'd never felt anything quite like it.

'Don't close your eyes,' he said thickly as he began to move inside her.

She didn't. They just grew wider and wider.

He kept his rhythm slow, withdrawing as far as possible before surging back into her as deep as he could go. His eyes didn't leave hers. He saw the pleasure build in them. And the tension. A tension he also felt.

A groan escaped his lips when her flesh began squeezing his, gripping it for dear life.

Dear God, don't let me come before her.

'Reece,' she said suddenly, her voice choked.

He stopped moving.

'No, no,' she moaned. 'Don't stop. Don't stop.'

He smiled. 'Whatever you say, Babe. Move with me this time. Go with the flow.'

In no time she came, her hips lifting from the bed as her body splintered apart.

Answering cries burst from Reece's throat. His shoulders shook. His back arched. His mind exploded, along with his body.

And it was whilst her flesh was milking his, over and over, that Reece realised something even more wonderful than the experience they'd just shared.

Today was the day Alanna had marked on the kitchen calendar with the biggest red circle. Today was the day when she was most likely to conceive.

She might never remember him. She might never love him. But after tonight, she was going to have his baby.

Reece was sure of it.

CHAPTER FOURTEEN

ALANNA woke with a start. And total recall.

'Oh!' she cried out, her heart racing with joy and relief. 'Oh, thank you, God.'

She could hardly believe it. She could remember everything!

Better still, all the confusion and worry that had been pressing in on her the last few days was totally gone. She no longer felt afraid. She no longer felt as if she didn't know who she was. She was her old self again.

Reece! She had to tell Reece!

But his side of the bed was empty and...

'Heavens!' she exclaimed on seeing the time on the bedside clock. Nine-fifteen.

Her excitement was dampened a little as she realised Reece had left for work. She had so wanted to tell him.

But then she saw his business card propped up against the side of the clock.

It wasn't the first time Reece had left her a note this way. Alanna snatched it up and turned it over.

'Glad to see you sleeping so well,' she read aloud. 'Will ring to check up on you around lunch-time. Take it easy. Love Reece.'

She sighed her pleasure in the note, her gaze travelling back from the clock to where his body had lain next to her, the imprint of his head still in the pillow.

Had it been his tender lovemaking that had done the trick? Broken through that veil of fear that she'd been living under since their car accident? Made her really relax and have such a sound sleep?

It must have been that.

Reece was going to be so glad. It couldn't have been easy being married to a wife who didn't remember him. Yet he'd been incredibly kind and sensitive.

She had to ring him. Tell him. Thank him.

Yet when she reached for the phone, an unexpected shyness overwhelmed Alanna. Her stomach went all fluttery and she found herself blushing as she recalled the way she'd acted last night.

One moment weeping with fear, the next clinging to Reece like a vine, quivering with a passion that had been as urgent as it had been powerful. Stunningly powerful.

Stunning, but not totally surprising, Alanna conceded.

She'd been having sexual feelings for Reece earlier in the evening, when he'd been totally dressed, not half naked in bed with her, holding her close and stroking her so sensually. By the time he'd kissed her, she could not have said no if her life had depended on it.

At the time, she'd been a bit shocked by her feelings. Now that she had her memory back, however, Alanna happily blamed her physical responses to Reece on her subconscious mind. Last weekend, after the wedding, he had finally tapped into the woman she probably would have become if Darko hadn't entered her life.

That woman had still been there, despite her memory loss, her newly liberated libido ripe and ready for more lovemaking. There was no need to feel awkward about it this morning, she told herself. Or embarrassed in the slightest.

If she were frankly honest, it had been a wonderful experience. Reece had been wonderful. There was no getting around that fact. Her mother had been right when…

'Oh, my God!' Alanna burst out. Her mother. Her poor mother.

Alanna groaned as she swept up the phone. Ringing Reece would have to wait. She had to ring her mother first and apologise.

'Mum, I'm so sorry!' Alanna blurted out as soon as her mother answered.

'Alanna!' Her mother sounded both relieved and delighted. 'You've got your memory back!'

'Yes. When I woke up this morning, everything was back to normal. Oh, Mum, do you forgive me?'

'Don't be silly, dear. Reece explained the situation and I understood entirely.'

'I do hope so. I hate to think I might have hurt you. You were so good to me when I came home after Darko's death. If it hadn't been for you I don't know what would have become of me.'

'You would have been fine. You're very strong, Alanna.'

'How can you say that? I stayed married to a pig for three years. I should have left him.'

'You loved him.'

'Only in the beginning…'

'You and I know why you didn't leave him, Alanna. You have to go through something like that to understand.'

'I suppose so. I just wish that..'

'Come on, now,' her mother interrupted. 'Don't start going over old ground. You've moved way past that. You have a good life now, and a very good husband. Reece really cares about you, Alanna. Forget the past and concentrate on the present, and the future.'

'I'll do that, Mum,' Alanna said, and glanced at the clock again. Twenty to ten. Suddenly, alarm bells began to ring in her brain. 'Oh, my goodness, I just remembered I have a visitor coming soon and I'm not even dressed.'

What an understatement! She was stark naked. Another reminder of her behaviour the previous night.

'Off you go, then,' her mother was saying. 'Glad to see that you're back to your old self. Give my love to Reece when you speak to him.'

'I'll do that, Mum. Bye,' she said, and hung up.

She had twenty minutes before Natalie arrived.

Not long.

So what was she doing lying back down in the bed, angling herself into the imprint of Reece's body and thinking about how it had felt when he'd made love to her last night? She could almost feel him now, thrusting deep into her, pulling back oh, so slowly, then thrusting deep again.

Her breath quickened. Her belly tightened. Her hands curled into fists by her sides.

Suddenly, she didn't want to ring him. She wanted to tell him in person. She wanted to be with him.

Tonight was too long to wait.

But first she would have to throw some clothes on and get rid of Natalie. That shouldn't take too long. After all, the reason for Natalie's visit was no longer relevant. Alanna knew exactly what kind of woman she'd been when she went to Wives Wanted.

A woman who had finally moved on from victim to survivor. A woman whom she was proud to be. A woman who'd decided what she wanted out of the rest of her life and was determined to get it.

Financial security. A physically attractive husband who respected her.

And a baby.

Alanna sat bolt upright.

A baby!

She didn't bother with clothes. She bolted downstairs, charging into the kitchen. On the wall next to the fridge was a calendar, one where she jotted down appointments and social obligations, plus the days she was most likely to conceive.

Her heart leapt into her mouth when she saw that yesterday had a big red circle around it, preceded by two days with little red circles around them, and two days with little circles afterwards.

Last night had been the very best night for them to make a baby!

Had Reece known that?

Possibly not. He wasn't as wrapped in having a baby as she was. Alanna sometimes got the feeling he was just going along with her plans for a family to please her.

A quiver of sheer joy rippled down her spine as she stared once more at that big red circle.

Maybe she shouldn't say anything. Not yet. For one thing, she didn't want to start getting her hopes up again.

But she had a good feeling about last night. A very good feeling.

Her hands lifted to rub softly over her stomach.

'Are you in there, my darling?' she whispered. 'Yes, you are, aren't you? It's Mummy here. Daddy's at work at the moment but we're going in to visit him soon. We're going on a ferry,' she rattled on more loudly as she whirled and hurried from the room. 'It's much quicker than driving. I hope you don't get seasick…'

Natalie eased her car into the kerb outside the Diamond house right on ten. Punctuality was a virtue of hers. Not that it got her anywhere these days. No one ever seemed to be on time for anything. When she was, and complained of the tardiness of others, she was accused of being anally retentive, or some such gobbledegook.

'The trouble with you,' her one true love had once said to her, 'is that you take life far too seriously.'

Possibly, that was true. But she didn't think it was unreasonable at the time to go ape when she discovered that the man she'd wasted the best years of her life on turned out to be married, with two children.

Natalie had begun Wives Wanted three years ago as therapy for herself, more than a means of making money. She gained a savage satisfaction every time she matched one of her female clients with a man who would, not only marry her, but give her children and provide for them all in style.

There'd been a time when she'd entertained the hope of finding such a man for herself.

Unfortunately, the experience of a grand passion betrayed had given her once softer personality a hard and very cynical edge that men didn't find attractive.

So it looked as if she was condemned to spend the rest of her days playing matchmaker.

A job she did very well, she thought as she pressed the front door bell. The Diamonds were only one of her many successes.

When no one came to the door, Natalie rang the bell again. Maybe the cleaner had the vacuum on. Or was upstairs. The house was simply huge! Alanna had certainly done very well for herself.

This time, the front door was yanked open reasonably quickly. But not by the cleaner. Alanna stood there, wearing jeans and looking utterly gorgeous, despite not having a scrap of make-up on.

'I'm so sorry to have dragged you out all this way

for nothing, Natalie,' she said with a wide smile. 'You've no idea what's happened. I woke up less than an hour ago from a simply fantastic night's sleep and it's back. My memory.'

'Well, isn't that marvelous?' Natalie said, genuinely pleased for her. She liked Alanna. 'Reece must be happy, too.'

'I haven't had the chance to tell him yet.'

Natalie was taken aback. Almost an hour ago, hadn't she said? Couldn't she have picked up the phone and called? The man *loved* her.

Damn it all, didn't she know how rare that was?

Natalie was tempted to tell her. But, of course, she didn't. A promise was a promise. And Reece was right. Alanna didn't want to be loved.

Natalie understood the reasons behind this. And empathised with it to a degree. Brandon had claimed to love her till the cows had come home. And she'd believed him. Believed everything he'd told all, all his excuses for not spending more time with her. Plus his reasons for delaying their marriage.

All lies.

Okay, so he hadn't physically hurt her. But the damage to her psyche had been enormous.

She would find it hard to believe that a man really loved her ever again.

Alanna, however, was *afraid* of being loved. Natalie could appreciate her fears. But it seemed a shame. Reece was such a nice man.

'Yes, I know what you're thinking,' Alanna said

swiftly. 'Why haven't I rung Reece already? The thing is...I want to tell him in person.'

Natalie blinked her surprise. 'That's a bit romantic for you, isn't it?'

She'd sussed out Alanna's personality when she'd interviewed her at length. They were sisters in cynicism when it came to romance.

Alanna laughed. 'I feel romantic today,' came her breezy reply.

The sheer happiness shining in her eyes stunned Natalie.

And then the penny dropped.

Did Alanna realise she'd fallen in love with her husband? Should she risk Reece's anger and say something now about his loving her back?

'Would you think me horribly rude if I didn't ask you in?' Alanna said before Natalie could make up her mind what to do for the best. 'I want to make myself presentable, then catch the next ferry. I only have forty minutes.'

Natalie decided that Alanna would discover the truth herself in time. There was no need for her to extend her matchmaking services to outright meddling.

If Natalie had known what was to transpire later that day, she might have decided differently.

'No, don't worry,' she answered. 'Go get ready. Glad you've got your memory back, Alanna. Give my regards to Reece when you see him.'

'I'll do that. And thanks again, Natalie. Sorry about this.'

'No need to apologise. I understand. Totally.'

CHAPTER FIFTEEN

THE breeze off the harbour ruffled Alanna's hair. But she didn't care. Her hair was pretty wind-proof, needing only a quick brush through to settle her natural waves back into place.

She was standing on the foredeck of the ferry, wishing it would go faster. She couldn't wait to tell Reece she remembered him, and their marriage, and everything!

It wasn't till the ferry docked at Circular Quay and she was moving down the gangway that Alanna realised Reece might not *be* in his office. Admittedly, he was between building projects at the moment, but that didn't mean he might not have dashed out to inspect a site he was thinking of buying. Or have left for lunch with some architect he was courting. Or engineer. Or client.

He was always doing that.

Still, it was a little early for lunch. Reece rarely ate before one. It was only noon and his building was just a short walk away. Hopefully, she'd find him sitting behind his desk.

But the possibility that he might not be there took some of the wind out of Alanna's sails. She hastened her step, oblivious of the second glances she received from every male who passed her by.

Frustration set in when the lights turned red on the corner opposite Reece's building, leaving her to tap her foot impatiently against the kerb.

Her eyes lifted to the twelfth floor as she waited, willing Reece to be there. Of course, she could always catch him on his mobile if he wasn't, but telling him over the phone just wouldn't be the same.

At last the lights turned green and she dashed forward, her long legs carrying her as quickly as they could with what she was wearing.

The outfit she'd chosen to meet Reece in was quite new. A chocolate suede suit that had a short, tight skirt and a three-quarter-length jacket, which she had left undone. Underneath she wore a lightweight polo in a caramel colour, which clung to her figure and made her small breasts look bigger. Her shoes were ankle-height black boots. Her natty handbag was black as well, with stylish wooden handles.

Her make-up was minimal. She only ever wore a skin-coloured sunscreen during the day. Her lipstick today was a bronze gloss and her eye-shadow a smoky green that matched her eyes. A touch of black mascara and that was it.

Alanna's heart was thudding in her chest by the time she stepped up onto the kerb on the other side of the street. Rushing plus the anticipation of seeing Reece again had put her into a highly excitable state. She hurried past the trendy coffee shop that sat right on the corner..and which she'd gone to occasionally with Reece..pushing through the revolving glass doors that led into his building.

She was crossing the expanse of black and white tiled floor, heading for the bank of lifts at the back of the cavernous foyer, when an idle glance to her right sent her heart skittering to a halt, much the same way as her legs did.

For there, sitting just behind the mainly glass wall that separated the foyer from the coffee shop, sat her husband. With a woman. A blonde woman.

Not Katie. Alanna wouldn't have minded Reece having coffee with Katie.

The sight of him sitting opposite *this* blonde, however, had the hairs on the back of her neck standing upright.

For it was Kristine. Reece's ex-fiancée.

Alanna had never met Kristine, but she'd come across a photo of her early in her marriage to Reece. It had been sitting on Reece's desk. Not framed or anything. But not hidden, either. When she'd asked Reece who it was, he'd told her without a trace of guilt.

At the time, she hadn't overly cared that he kept a photo of his ex-fiancée. That was his personal and private business. The Alanna who'd gone into marriage with her head and not her heart wasn't about to tell her husband what he could and couldn't do.

But she'd taken a good, long, hard look at the woman he'd been madly in love with, curious over what she looked like.

Very sexy, that was what. One of those flashy blondes with big hair and big eyes and big lips.

Alanna could not stop staring at her through the

glass wall, her eyes glued to the way Kristine's hand was stretched out across the café table, covering one of Reece's in a highly intimate fashion. He wasn't pulling it away, either.

The emotional storm that immediately brewed up within Alanna's chest took her breath away. Her jealousy was fierce, as was her hurt.

He was *her* husband. *Her* man. *Her* lover.

She would not share him. She *loved* him.

The realisation floored her. Then appalled her.

She didn't want to love him, especially not in the way that evoked such a dark and powerful jealousy.

It was a curse, that kind of love. It warped minds and destroyed lives.

But even as she told herself not to be jealous her jealousy increased, fuelling an explosive anger within her tightened chest.

Yet Reece wasn't really doing anything wrong, she tried telling herself. Just having coffee with an old flame. And in a public place, for heaven's sake. It wasn't as though he'd whipped the woman off to a hotel room for the afternoon.

And it was Kristine who was doing the pawing. She was probably one of those touchy-feelie women.

Then let her be touchy-feelie with some other man, came the savage thought. *Not mine!*

The temptation to barge in there and slap the bitch's face was acute. *Too* acute.

Horror that she was acting the way Darko had acted propelled Alanna across to the lifts where she practically fell into one, grateful that it was empty. She didn't want anyone seeing the ugliness in her face.

For jealousy *was* ugly. Ugly and destructive.

By the time the lift opened on the twelfth floor, Alanna had pulled herself together sufficiently to walk into the head office of Diamond Enterprises in what she hoped was her usual manner.

'Hello, Katie,' she said breezily as she came through the door.

The receptionist looked shocked. 'Alanna! My God, you *know* me!'

'Yes. I've got my memory back. Isn't it wonderful?'

'It certainly is. When did this happen?'

'When I woke up this morning. I was going to ring Reece, but then I thought I'd come in and surprise him.'

Alanna tried not to read anything in the flash of worry that zoomed into Katie's eyes.

'He…er…isn't in his office at the moment. He stepped out for some coffee. But he should be back soon. I'll give him a buzz on his mobile and tell him you're here.'

Alanna could feel her smile turning brittle. Were women employees always this protective of their bosses? Did Katie lie for Reece on a regular basis? What other times had she covered for Reece since their marriage? Maybe he'd been having affairs behind her back all along.

It was possible.

He didn't love her, after all.

'Yes, please do that,' she said, hoping she sounded polite and not as vicious as she was suddenly feeling towards the woman. 'I'll wait for him in his office,' she added, and headed straight in there, closing the door firmly behind her.

Best she be alone for a while with the way she was feeling. She couldn't trust herself to continue to act normally.

Yet she *must* by the time Reece arrived. To start questioning him over where he'd been and whom he'd been with would be the kiss of death to their relationship. He would not tolerate such behaviour. He might leave her.

Losing Reece was an even worse fate than loving him. She had to learn to hide her love, and to control her jealousy. Really, she had no evidence that he'd been unfaithful to her, either with Kristine or any other woman.

But if he were totally innocent, wouldn't he *tell* her he'd just been having coffee with his ex?

Hopefully, when he arrived, he would.

She spent some time brushing her hair, then pacing the office, then staring out of the window at the view. But all she could think about was how long it was taking Reece to tear himself away from his beloved Kristine. He was only just downstairs, after all. How long did it take to say goodbye and get himself up here?

Finally, the door to the office burst open and there he was, looking as drop-dead gorgeous as ever, his

handsome face beaming, his eyes showing nothing
but delight at her visiting him here.

'Alanna! How beautiful you look today!' he said
as he closed the door and came forward. 'Better still,
you've got your memory back, haven't you?'

Alanna stiffened a little as he slid his arms around
her back, underneath her jacket.

'How did you know?' she threw up at him. 'Did
Katie tell you?'

Reece grinned and pulled her closer. 'Nope. I put
two and two together. After all, how else could you
have known where my office was?'

'The business card you left me had the address on
it,' she pointed out rather frostily.

He looked startled for a second, then he laughed.
'Stop teasing me, you saucy minx. You've remembered everything all right. Why else would you have
come here to me in person, dressed like this? You're
my old Alanna again. As well as my new Alanna,'
he murmured, his voice dropping low and husky.

His kissing her made her forget her jealousy for a
few moments, but the second his lips lifted it was
back with a vengeance, digging away at her.

'I was disappointed when you weren't here,' she
heard herself say. 'Where were you?'

'Just downstairs, having coffee.'

'All by yourself?'

'No. I was with an old friend.'

'Oh? Who?'

'No one you know.'

His twisting of the truth was like a dagger in her heart, making it bleed tears of blood.

'What say I take you somewhere swish for lunch?' he offered. 'The Rockpool. I'll get Katie to make us a reservation.'

Alanna bit her bottom lip. This was it. One of those moments when you had to decide the path your life was going to take. She could confront Reece about having seen him with Kristine. Or turn a blind eye.

It was then that she remembered the baby. The baby she was almost sure she'd conceived last night. A baby deserved two parents.

'Alanna?' Reece said. 'Is there something wrong?'

Alanna made up her mind. 'Not at all. I was just wondering if you realised last night was the most fertile time of my cycle.'

'I did, indeed,' he replied, the warm glitter in his eyes reassuring her.

Maybe he'd just run into Kristine by accident. Maybe his sidestepping her identity meant nothing.

And maybe not…

'You *really* want to have children with me, Reece?'

'What a strange thing to say! Of course I do. Come on, let's go have a fabulous lunch to celebrate you remembering everything.'

Alanna felt reasonably happy as Reece swept her out of his office and through Reception. If only she hadn't taken that last glance over her shoulder at Katie when she said goodbye.

The receptionist now had an extremely relieved

look on her face, as if some major crisis had just passed.

What crisis could possibly have just passed, unless it was that the boss's wife hadn't found out that the boss was still meeting his ex, and that.. oh, God, not that. Surely not that. He couldn't still be madly in love with Kristine, could he?

Alanna could cope with Reece not loving her. But not with his being madly in love with someone else.

CHAPTER SIXTEEN

SHE wasn't quite her old self again, Reece realised as he watched her through lunch. She was too bright. And way too bubbly.

The Alanna he'd married was a coolly confident creature. Very sure of herself. She wasn't a try-hard.

Alanna's recent memory loss had changed her.

Was it because the dark memories of her marriage to Darko were now fresher in her mind? Maybe she was trying to push them aside too quickly by pretending to be more extroverted than usual. Maybe she was afraid of slipping back into the victim mentality that she'd lived with for so long, and which must have taken an enormous effort of will to overcome.

Alanna had no idea how much he admired her for what she'd accomplished in her life. To throw off such a past was not easy.

By comparison, *his* past had been very easy to throw off.

Seeing Kristine again today had underlined that fact.

What a stupid, shallow, superficial female she was, thinking she could turn up at his office, just like that, and get him back. He'd only taken her downstairs for a cup of coffee because she'd started acting like a fool, throwing her silly arms around him and trying to kiss him, right in full view of Katie.

As it was, she'd still grabbed his hand over coffee, holding on so hard that it had been easier to leave it there than pull it away. His only emotion as he'd listened to her abject apologies had been amazement. Amazement that he'd ever thought he'd loved her.

When she'd claimed that she still loved him and she *knew* he still loved her, Reece had put her straight in no uncertain terms. At which point, she'd started to cry.

Katie's phone call to say that Alanna was in the office had been a godsend. It had still taken him a few minutes to extricate himself without Kristine making a big scene. He'd ordered a taxi for her and put her in it, making sure that she couldn't do anything crazy like follow him up to the office. He might not be able to tell Alanna that he loved her, but he didn't want her thinking he was being unfaithful to her.

Women were sometimes quick to jump to conclusions like that, especially where another attractive woman was concerned. As much as Reece didn't think Kristine was a patch on Alanna, she was still a sexy-looking woman. Not the kind of ex you wanted floating around your office when the wife you loved was there.

'I simply don't know what to order for dessert,' Alanna said with a shrug of her slender shoulders as she inspected the menu.

'Something delicious and fattening,' Reece advised.

Her upward glance projected instant worry. 'You think I'm too skinny?'

Reece smothered a groan as he recalled Darko used to tell her she was too skinny.

'Not at all,' he replied. 'But you might be eating for two, remember?'

True joy gleamed back at him.

Now this was a subject that always made her happy.

Babies.

'I don't want to get my hopes up too soon,' she said.

'Why not? Life is all about hope, isn't it?' He hoped that one day she'd fall in love with him. Judy had told him the other night her daughter had a lot of love to give, which was why she was so keen about having children.

Hopefully, Alanna might have some left over for him one day, too.

The sound of his cell phone ringing made Reece swear under his breath. He should have turned the darned thing off.

Pulling it out of his pocket, he flipped it open and put it to his ear. 'Yes?' he said rather impatiently.

'Jake here, Reece. Sorry to bother you at lunch, but you remember that land up at the Gold Coast you've been wanting to buy for ages? I just got a tip from a friend that it's coming on the market this weekend. It's being advertised in tomorrow's paper. If you fly up there today, you could snap it up before anyone else gets the chance.'

'Today,' Reece repeated, glancing over the table at Alanna.

'We're talking prime real estate, boss. Right on the beach. It won't last, even in the present climate.'

'Yes. I know that. But today's almost over. What about tomorrow?'

'There are no early-morning flights to the Gold Coast.'

'I see.'

'Shall I get Katie to book you an afternoon flight, then? And a car? And an apartment at Coolangatta Court?'

Reece didn't want to leave Alanna alone tonight. At the same time, a chance like this might not come again. If he was going to have a family he had to think about the future. They'd be financially secure for life if he bought this land. On top of that, it would give him more money to do good work with. God had really come through for him today, so he had to reciprocate.

'Okay,' he agreed.

'Great.' Jake said, and hung up.

Reece pulled a face as he slipped his phone back into his pocket. 'This is unfortunate timing,' he said. 'I have to go away. This afternoon. To the Gold Coast. It should be for only one night, but possibly two if I don't clinch the deal tomorrow.'

He almost asked her to go with him. But he never had before. She might think it odd.

'Oh,' Alanna said, a momentary cloud crossing her

eyes. But then her eyes grew bright again. 'Oh, well, it can't be helped, I suppose. That's your job. I might ask Mum to come down. I did ring her, you know, and apologise for my not wanting to see her, or talk to her.'

'That's good. I was a bit worried about that.'

'No need. Mum understood. Look, under the circumstances I think I'll skip dessert,' she said, putting the menu down on the tablecloth. 'You'll want to be getting home to pack.'

'I don't think I'll have the time. I'll use the emergency bag of clothes I keep at the office. I should get going.' He called for the waiter and the bill. 'I'll get them to order you a taxi as well.'

'All right,' she agreed.

Five minutes later Reece was waving her off and resenting what he had once appreciated. He didn't want Alanna being so damned agreeable any more. He didn't want her not really caring about where he went and what he did whilst he was there.

He could have sworn that the Alanna he'd discovered last weekend.. and last night.. might have insisted on coming with him.

She was an enigma, all right. There again, she always had been. Even now, knowing everything about her, he still didn't totally understand her.

But he did love her. More than he could have ever thought possible. He hated leaving her, even for one night.

He'd close that damn deal tomorrow and get back by tomorrow night, or his name wasn't Reece Diamond!

CHAPTER SEVENTEEN

ALANNA'S agitation increased as the afternoon wore on. She could not settle to anything. She paced around the house, still wearing the same clothes she'd worn into town. All she could think about was Reece up on the Gold Coast, not to buy land, but to have a romantic rendezvous with Kristine.

It was too much of a coincidence, his having coffee with her and then dashing off like that the same day.

Jealousy bored away at Alanna like an insidious worm.

Yet she hated jealousy. Hated it with a vengeance.

Darko had been jealous all the time, right from the moment he'd discovered on their wedding night that she wasn't a virgin. Jealousy had eaten away at him, making him irrational and violent in the end.

'But this is different,' Alanna muttered away to herself. 'Darko had no reason to be jealous. I do!'

Because Reece didn't love her. That was the trouble.

Alanna moaned. She couldn't bear the thought of her husband being in that woman's arms. Not for a minute, let alone a night. Maybe two.

But then another thought came to her. Maybe this wasn't the first time. Reece had gone away a lot during their relatively short marriage. Maybe Kristine had been going with him for a while. Or all along.

Then why had he married *her*?

The conversation she'd had with Mike last Saturday night popped into her head. Mike knew much more about Reece's relationship with Kristine than she did.

She would *make* him tell her what he knew, Alanna resolved as she raced into the kitchen, snatched up the phone and pressed number two. The numbers of all Reece's best friends were programmed in. Richard was number one. Mike number two.

Frustration set in when Mike didn't answer straight away. He did work from home, but maybe he was out. If it kept on ringing, in a moment it would cut into his answering machine. If it did, she would just hang up.

'Mike Stone.'

'Oh, Mike. Thank God you're home.'

'Alanna? Is that you?'

'Yes, yes, I..'

'You've got your memory back!' he exclaimed.

Alanna grimaced. 'Reece told you about that, did he?'

'Well, of course. The man was worried sick.'

'Was he really?' she said, far too drily.

Her tone brought silence from the other end of the line.

'I don't want to talk about that,' she went on abruptly. 'Look, Mike, remember last Saturday night, when you wouldn't tell me about what happened the day Kristine left Reece?'

'Yeah. Why?'

'You have to tell me now. I have to know.'

'Alanna, I..'

'I think he's gone away with her. With Kristine.'

'*What?* I don't believe that.'

'I saw them having coffee together today in town and they looked very cosy indeed. I'd gone in there to tell Reece my memory had come back. Then later, over lunch, he gets this phone call and he suddenly decides he has to go to the Gold Coast for a day or two on business. I don't believe in that kind of co-incidence, Mike. He still loves her, doesn't he?'

'No, damn it. I don't think he does.'

'Tell me what happened that day,' she insisted.

Mike sighed.

'Tell me, Mike. And tell me why you think he married me. You know. I know you do.'

'Hell, Alanna, that's all in the past. Things have changed since then. *Reece* has changed.'

'Mike, stop trying to protect the man. Give it to me straight. I can cope with the truth. I can't cope with lies.'

More silence from the other end.

'Mike, *please*,' she begged.

'Oh, all right,' he said with a disgruntled sigh. 'But I still think you're barking up the wrong tree.'

He told her how Kristine had made love to Reece that final day, all day, in ways that most men only fantasised about. Afterwards, she'd risen from his bed, dressed, then coolly told him that she was leaving him and that when he was lying alone in his bed at night he could think about her doing all those things with her new lover.

The last thing she'd said as she'd walked out the door was that she still loved him.

'But why did she leave him if she still loved him?' Alanna asked, confused.

'Because he wouldn't sell this huge parcel of land he'd sunk all his money into,' Mike explained. 'The rates alone were gradually sending him bankrupt. He could have sold it.. at a loss.. but he wouldn't. He told me he knew it would be worth a fortune in another year or two. He didn't mind being poor for a while. But Kristine did. She wanted the good life. If she'd only waited with him, she could have had both. Reece *and* the good life.'

'I see. And his marriage to me?' Alanna asked, although she had a sinking feeling what Mike was going to say.

'In the beginning, I think it was a kind of revenge on Kristine. To show her he'd moved on without her, in every way. I guess he wanted to make her jealous, too. As jealous as she'd made him.'

'Jealous?' she repeated a bit blankly.

'You're a very beautiful woman, Alanna. More beautiful than Kristine. It would have been a blow to her vanity to see Reece married to someone as stunning as you.'

Alanna's heart sank. So that was why he dressed

her the way he did. Why he was always so pleased when their photos were in the papers and magazines.

All to spite Kristine.

'I'm sure Reece doesn't think like that now,' Mike went on, an urgency on his voice. 'Remember how jealous he was of you the other night when I danced with you? He doesn't give a damn about Kristine any more. I'd put my money on it. Look, let me ring Reece on his mobile and talk to him. I'll bet he..'

'No,' Alanna cut in firmly. 'No, please don't do that. This is my affair, Mike. Or possibly Reece's affair,' she added with a cold little laugh. 'I have to deal with it myself. Promise me you'll stay out of it.'

'But..'

'*Promise* me!'

'I didn't realise you could be so tough.'

'I'm a survivor too, Mike.'

Brave words. She didn't feel like much of a survivor at this moment. More like another victim.

But only temporarily. Because she would not live with fear again, even if that fear was only in her mind and heart. She certainly would not live with jealousy, especially her own. She'd rather confront the truth than ever live like that.

The time had come to take action.

'Bye, Mike,' she said.

'Before you go, promise *me* something.'

'What?'

'Call me when you find out you're wrong.'

CHAPTER EIGHTEEN

RECCE couldn't work out where Alanna was. He'd rung her at home as soon as he'd checked in. But there was no answer. When he'd tried her mobile, she had it turned off. He'd left a message, but so far there'd been no answer from her, which was odd.

They'd never lived in each other's pockets, but he always kept in touch when he was away. And Alanna never went out on a Thursday night. Not alone, anyway.

Maybe she'd gone to the gym for a long workout to make up for the days she'd missed. Or maybe she'd decided to drive home to visit her mother, instead of the other way around.

Reece contemplated ringing Judy to find out, but decided that was carrying things a bit far. He didn't want to start acting like that creep Alanna had been married to, checking up on her all the time.

No. He'd have a shower, then go to bed and read. He'd picked up one of those blockbusters at the airport and started it during the flight up.

Reece had just switched off the water in the shower when he thought he heard someone knocking on the door. Pulling on the hotel bathrobe, he hurried through the bedroom into the sitting area, finger-combing his wet hair back from his face on the way.

Someone was very definitely knocking at his door.

'Who is it?' he demanded through the door, puzzled. Hotel employees always announced themselves. But no one was saying Room Service, or Housekeeping.

'It's me, Reece,' came the truly amazing reply. 'Alanna.'

'Alanna!' Reece whipped off the security chain and pulled open the door.

And there she was, looking beautiful but extremely uptight.

He didn't know whether to be delighted, or worried.

'What on earth are you doing here?' he blurted out.

'I caught the eight-twenty flight,' she said, all the while looking him up and down in the strangest fashion.

Not sexually. Assessingly.

'Yes, I can see that,' he said with a slightly awkward laugh. 'But why?'

'Aren't you going to invite me in?'

Her chilly tone stunned him.

She didn't wait for any invitation. She just forged past him, turning left and heading straight for the bedroom.

And then it twigged. She thought he was here with someone. She'd followed him, hoping to catch him out with some woman.

Bloody hell!

Reece banged the door shut and charged after her. By this time, she'd reached the bedroom, which was a typical hotel room, with few places to hide a partner in adultery. Reece watched her frown as she glanced around.

'Perhaps you'd better check out the bathroom,' he threw at her. 'She might be hiding behind the shower curtain.'

'If there was a stupid shower curtain,' he muttered under his breath when she actually did as he suggested.

By the time Alanna returned to the bedroom, Reece was almost gratified to see that all the blood had drained from her face, leaving her skin even more pale than usual.

'You're alone,' she said, her eyes wide with surprise.

'Are you sure?' he ground out. 'She might be running late. Whoever *she* is.'

'Kristine, of course. The woman you're still in love with.'

'Kristine! Are you mad? I'm not still in love with Kristine.'

Colour zoomed back into her cheeks. 'Don't lie to me. I saw you together. Today. Holding hands.'

'She was holding *my* hand. I can't stand the woman.'

Alanna's eyes flared wide. 'You can't?'

'No. I...'

Reece broke off and just stared at her.

For the rest of his life, he would never forget this wondrous moment, when Alanna's uncharacteristic actions suddenly made sense and he realised that his dearest wish had come true.

'You were jealous,' he said, his voice as stunned as his suddenly joyous soul.

Her face twisted, her eyes tormented. 'I... I... I was wrong.'

'No, not wrong, my darling,' he said as he came forward and drew her into his arms. 'You've never been more right in all your life. You love me, don't you?'

'Oh, God,' she cried. 'I'm such a fool.'

'If you're a fool, then I'm one too. Because I love you.'

Her eyes turned to liquid pools as she stared up at him. 'You love me?' she choked out.

'With all my heart. I nearly died last Sunday when I thought you were hurt. Then, when you couldn't remember me, I was in sheer hell.'

'But you were so wonderful!'

'That was the new me.'

'The new you? What do you mean by that?'

Reece felt a little embarrassed, telling her about his bargains with God. But he did it all the same.

He was touched that she was so touched.

'But you always *were* a good man,' she complimented him.

'Not good enough for you, Alanna. You deserve the very best.'

'Oh, Reece, that's so sweet.'

'I've been dying to tell you all week that I love you, but I was afraid to.'

'*You*, Reece? Afraid? You're never afraid.'

'I was afraid of losing you, my darling. You always said that you never wanted to be loved again. When I realised last weekend that I'd fallen in love with you, I was worried sick.'

'Oh, Reece…'

'I wanted to ask you to come away with me today,' he told her. 'But I didn't dare. I was afraid you might think it odd. I had no idea you'd seen me with Kristine. Or that you might think what you did.'

Her smile was softly rueful. 'If you were in hell last Sunday, then I was in hell today. When I saw you in that coffee shop with that woman, it took all of my will-power not to charge in there. I've never experienced that kind of jealousy before, Reece. I wanted to do dreadful things to her. I can't tell you how appalled I felt at the time. Appalled and ashamed. I hate jealousy of any kind.'

'I can understand that,' he said softly, though privately thinking he'd rather liked hers.

'Jealousy is a terrible thing,' she went on. 'It feeds on itself and becomes more and more irrational. I mean…you weren't doing anything wrong in that coffee shop. Just having coffee. And you're right. I could see it was her hand covering yours, not the other way around. Yet the more I tried telling myself you were totally innocent, the more I started seeing deception in everything you said and did, especially when you took so long to come back after Katie contacted you.'

'I was worried that Kristine might follow me up to the office and cause a scene in front of you, so I called her a taxi and waited with her till she was safely gone.'

'It's all right, Reece. You don't have to explain yourself.'

But Reece felt he did owe her an explanation. Otherwise she might always worry and wonder. He knew he would, if Alanna's ex were still alive and well.

'Do you know, Kristine seriously thought she could just show up in my life after all this time and get me back? She even imagined I was still in love with her. The woman has to be totally deranged!'

'But you did love her once,' Alanna pointed out. 'You were still in love with her when you married me.'

'I thought I was. But, looking back, I'm not sure that what I felt for Kristine was ever love. Frankly, I don't think I knew what real love was back then. I was too young, and way too selfish. But I know now, my darling,' he said, pulling his lovely Alanna even closer. 'It's what I feel for you. I adore you, Alanna. And I do so admire you. You are an incredible woman to survive what you survived with that monster. I can't imagine too many other women having the courage to move on and make a new life for yourself after what you went through. I feel so grateful that you chose me to trust, and to marry. I am one lucky man.'

She shook her head at him, her eyes shining. '*I'm* the lucky one. I never thought I would say I was happy to lose my memory, but I am saying it now. It made me step back and take a good look at the man I married. Having Darko fresh in my mind made me see why I chose you as my second husband. I think I've always loved you, Reece. I just didn't realise it till today. No, I subconsciously knew it last night, when you made love to me so beautifully. That's why I remembered everything when I woke this morning. Because it was safe to do so. You made me feel safe, Reece. That might not seem such a big deal, but it is to me.'

And there it was, that look he'd always wanted her to give him. The look of true love.

Reece's heart turned over.

'I'm so sorry I was jealous,' she said as she lowered her head to his chest, her arms tightening around him at the same time.

'I'm not,' Reece returned warmly. 'Because if you hadn't been, you wouldn't be here and we'd still be pretending not to love each other. Which wouldn't be a good idea,' Reece added with a smile in his voice, 'now that we've become parents.'

Her head whipped up, her eyes bright. 'You believe that, too?'

'Yes, I do.'

'We might be wrong.'

'Well, tonight's the second best night for you conceiving, you know. How about we make sure?'

Alanna was lying in Reece's arms afterwards, savouring the moment and thinking that happiness like this only came once in a lifetime. Then again, a man like Reece only came along once in a lifetime.

'Reece,' she said softly.

'Mmm?'

'I have to make a phone call.'

'What, *now*? At this hour?'

'Yes.'

'Who to?'

'Mike.'

'Mike!'

'Now none of that. We love each other and trust each other. We don't ever need to be jealous. I just have to tell Mike something. I promised him.'

'Promised him what?'

'You can listen in.'

'Oh, all right,' Reece grumbled, and reached for his mobile, flipping it open and pressing a couple of buttons.

'It's ringing his number,' he said by the time he handed it over.

'Mike Stone,' Mike finally answered in a gruff tone. 'This had better be important. It's bloody late and I was working.'

'It's important,' Alanna told him. 'You were right and I was wrong. Reece doesn't love Kristine. He loves me, almost as much as I love him. Now you can go back to work.'

'And you can go back to whatever you were doing,' Mike said with a low chuckle.

'Oh, yes,' she said, her eyes sparkling up at Reece as she handed him back the phone. 'I fully intend to.'

EPILOGUE

Positive. It was positive.

Alanna cried out her joy, then burst into tears.

Reece dashed into the bathroom, panic in his eyes.

'What is it? What's happened?'

Tears streamed down her face as she held the indicator out to him.

'I bought one of those home tests,' she choked out. 'It turned blue.'

'Is that good news or bad news?'

'It's wonderful news,' she sobbed, and grabbed a handful of tissues.

All of a sudden, Reece wanted to cry himself.

Alanna was having a baby. *His* baby.

He'd thought he wanted her to get pregnant just for her sake; to give her what she most wanted in the world. He hadn't realised how much it would mean to him on a personal level.

She smiled through her tears. 'You should see the look on your face.'

'I'm feeling unexpectedly overwhelmed,' he said faintly. 'I might have to lie down.'

'*I'm* the one having the baby.'

'I'm the one who gave it to you,' he retorted. 'Clearly, it's taken it out of me.'

'You poor thing,' she said, still smiling. 'But you

can't lie down. There isn't time. Richard and Holly will be here soon to look at the house.'

Richard and Holly had arrived home from their honeymoon the previous day, and were delighted with Reece's news that he'd found them just the house to buy.

'Needs a few renovations,' Reece had told his best friend over the phone last night. 'But it's a bargain at the price they're asking. Better yet, it's only three doors up from us!'

Reece couldn't wait to see his best friend again. *And* to tell him about the baby.

'You're right,' he said with a glance at his watch. 'They'll be here in less than ten minutes. Just time enough for you to ring your mother and me to ring mine.'

Ten minutes later, it was a beaming Reece and Alanna who answered the door to Richard and Holly.

It only took Richard a couple of minutes to see the change in his best friend and his lovely wife. Holly seemed to sense something, too.

'If I didn't know better,' Richard whispered to Holly as they followed Reece and Alanna into the house, 'I'd think *they* were the ones who'd just come back from their honeymoon.'

'I was thinking exactly the same thing,' Holly whispered back. 'Do you see the way they're looking at each other?'

'They've fallen in love,' Richard said.

'Madly, I'd say,' Holly agreed.

Just then, both Alanna and Reece stopped and

turned to face their friends. Reece slid his arm tightly around Alanna's waist and pulled her close.

'Before we have coffee or go along to see your new house, we have something to tell you,' he announced.

'You're pregnant,' Holly said, smiling at Alanna, who was positively glowing.

'Yes! How did you guess? I haven't put on any weight yet. I'm only a few weeks gone.'

'I only had to look into your face. I've never seen you so happy. You too, Reece.'

'We're very happy,' Reece replied. 'And very much in love.'

Both Richard and Holly laughed. 'We could see that, too,' they chorused.

'Mike's never going to believe this, you know,' Richard added ruefully.

'Oh, I think he will,' Alanna said. 'Mike's not quite the hard nut he pretends to be. It wouldn't surprise me if, one day, he falls in love himself.'

Richard and Reece looked at one another and roared with laughter. Holly and Alanna looked at one another, and smiled.

Look forward to all these ★ wonderful books this ★ Christmas

BETTY NEELS
MARGARET WAY
JESSICA STEELE

All I want for **Christmas**

Precious Gifts

Together for **Christmas**

Lynnette Kent & Sherryl Woods

Christmas

Jasmine Cresswell Kate Hoffmann
Tara Taylor Quinn

The **CHRISTMAS VISIT**

Margaret Moore
Gail Ranstrom
Terri Brisbin

SILHOUETTE
SNOWY NIGHTS

1005/01a

researching the cure

The facts you need to know:

- **One woman in nine** in the United Kingdom will develop breast cancer during her lifetime.

- Each year **40,700** women are newly diagnosed with breast cancer and around **12,800** women will die from the disease. However, survival rates are improving, with on average 77 per cent of women still alive five years later.

- **Men can also suffer from breast cancer**, although currently they make up less than one per cent of all new cases of the disease.

Britain has one of the highest breast cancer death rates in the world. Breast Cancer Campaign wants to understand why and do something about it. Statistics cannot begin to describe the impact that breast cancer has on the lives of those women who are affected by it and on their families and friends.

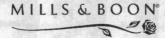

MILLS & BOON®

BCC/AD b

During the month of October Harlequin Mills & Boon will donate 10p from the sale of every Modern Romance™ series book to help Breast Cancer Campaign in *researching the cure.*

Breast Cancer Campaign's scientific projects look at improving diagnosis and treatment of breast cancer, better understanding how it develops and ultimately either curing the disease or preventing it.

Do your part to help

Visit <u>www.breastcancercampaign.org</u>

And make a donation today.

researching the cure

4 FREE

BOOKS AND A SURPRISE GIFT!

We would like to take this opportunity to thank you for reading this Mills & Boon® book by offering you the chance to take FOUR more specially selected titles from the Modern Romance™ series absolutely FREE! We're also making this offer to introduce you to the benefits of the Reader Service™—

- ★ **FREE home delivery**
- ★ **FREE gifts and competitions**
- ★ **FREE monthly Newsletter**
- ★ **Exclusive Reader Service offers**
- ★ **Books available before they're in the shops**

Accepting these FREE books and gift places you under no obligation to buy, you may cancel at any time, even after receiving your free shipment. Simply complete your details below and return the entire page to the address below. You don't even need a stamp!

YES! Please send me 4 free Modern Romance books and a surprise gift. I understand that unless you hear from me, I will receive 6 superb new titles every month for just £2.75 each, postage and packing free. I am under no obligation to purchase any books and may cancel my subscription at any time. The free books and gift will be mine to keep in any case.

P5ZED

Ms/Mrs/Miss/Mr ....Initials ....

BLOCK CAPITALS PLEASE

Surname ....

Address ....

....

....Postcode..........................

Send this whole page to:
UK: FREEPOST CN81, Croydon, CR9 3WZ